SOMETHING WAS HAPPENING . . .

"Felix—you've got to listen. What do you see coming through that door?"

Felix frowned. "Four young women, very gay, very sweet. Would that I had time . . ." His face was paling. "John, you're breaking my arm—"

I jerked my hand back. "They're aliens, Felix! The dog things I saw in the ravine. Look again and try to see them!" Felix tensed; an uncertain expression crept over his face. The first of the monstrosities quickened its pace, breaking into a clumsy gallop, closing now, red eyes glinting, the black tongue lolling from the side of the wide jaws as it cleared the last few yards and sprang. . . .

KEITH LAUMER

PLAGUE OF DEMONS

science fiction

A PLAGUE OF DEMONS

Copyright © 1965 by Keith Laumer. A shorter version of this novel appeared serially in IF Magazine, November-December, 1964.

Copyright © 1964 by Galaxy Publishing Corporation.

A Baen Book

Baen Enterprises
8-10 W. 36th Street
New York, N.Y. 10018

First Baen printing, September 1985

ISBN: 0-671-55982-6

Cover art by Wayne Barlowe

Printed in the United States of America

Distributed by
SIMON & SCHUSTER
MASS MERCHANDISE SALES COMPANY
1230 Avenue of the Americas
New York, N.Y. 10020

Chapter One

IT was ten minutes past high noon when I paid off my helicab, ducked under the air blast from the caged high-speed rotors as they whined back to speed, and looked around at the sun-scalded, dust-white, mob-noisy bazaar of the trucial camp-city of Tamboula, Republic of Free Algeria. Merchants' stalls were a clash of garish fabrics, the pastels of heaped fruit, the glitter of oriental gold thread and beadwork, the glint of polished Japanese lenses and finely-machined Swedish chromalloy, the subtle gleam of hand-rubbed wood, the brittle complexity of Hong Kong plastic—islands in the tide of humanity that elbowed, sauntered, bargained with shrill voices and waving hands or stood idly in patches of black shadow under rigged awnings all across the wide square. I made my way through the press, shouted at by hucksters, solicited by whining beggars and tattooed drabs, jostled by UN Security Police escorting officials of a dozen nations.

I emerged on a badly-paved street of starved royal palms, across from a row of fast-decaying buildings as cosmopolitan in style as the costumes around me. Above the cacophony of the mob, keening Arab music shrilled from cave-like openings redolent of goat and curry, vying with the PA-borne blare of Jump and Jitter, reflecting hectic lunch-hours behind the sweat-dewed glass fronts of the Café Parisien, Die Valkyrie, the Samovar, and the Chicago Snackery.

I crossed the street, dodging the iron-shod wheels of oxcarts, the scorching exhaust of jet-peds, the stinging dust-barrage of cushion cars—snorting one almost palpable stench from my nostrils just in time to catch a new and even riper one. Under a ten-foot glare-sign lettered ALHAMBRA ROOM in phony Arabic script, a revolving door thumped monotonously; I caught it and went through into a sudden gloom and silence. I crossed an unswept mosaic floor, went down three steps into an even darker room with a scatter of gaudy cushions and a gleam of gold filigree. I waved away a yard-square red and gold menu proffered by a nicely-rounded harem slave in a brief vest and transparent trousers. I took a stool at the long bar. A bare-chested three-hundred-pound eunuch with a cutlass, sash, and turban took my order, slid a frosty glass across the polished black marble. Behind a screen of gilded palm fronds, a small combo made reedy music.

I took a long draught; from the corner of my eye I saw a man slide onto the next stool. Casually, I angled the ring on my left forefinger; its specular surface reflected a narrow, tanned face with a bald forehead, peaked white eyebrows, a Kaiser Wilhelm mustache, and a satanic Vandyck. A pair of frosty blue eyes met mine for an instant in the tiny mirror.

"What's the get-up for, Felix?" I asked softly. "You traveling in hair-goods now?"

His eyelids flickered. For Felix Severance, that was equivalent to a yelp of astonishment. Then he gave me the trick wink that was service code for 'The Enemy May Be Listening.'

"Well, well, John Bravais, as I live and breathe," he said in his high-pitched voice. "Fancy meeting you here . . ."

We went through a ritual of hand pumping and when-did-I-see-you-last's, ordered second drinks, then moved over to a low table. He slipped a small gadget from a pocket, glanced around to see who was watching, then ran it over the light fixture, the salt and pepper shakers, the ashtray, babbling on:

"Martha's fine. Little Herbie had a touch of Chinese virus, and Charlotte broke a clavicle . . ." He went on point like a hunting dog, picked up a small *tabukuk* in the form of a frog-goddess, dropped it inconspicuously into his heavy briefcase.

"I heard you were going into mink farming," I said, carrying on the charade.

"Decided against it, Johnny." He checked the spice tray. "Too damned vicious; lousy example for little Lennie and Bertha and the others—" He finished the check, switched off the patter in midsentence, pocketed the spy-eye detector.

"Okay, Johnny," he said softly. "My little gem-dandy patented nose-counter says we're clean." He was looking me over with that quick glance of his that could count the pearls on a dowager's neck while he was bowing over her wrist. "Thanks for coming."

"I haven't run to fat yet, if that's what's bothering you," I said. "Now stop sizing me up and tell me what the false beard is all about. I heard you were here under an open cover as a UN medic."

"I'm afraid *Médecin-Major* de Salle attracted some unwelcome attention." He grinned. "It seems I broached security. I was advised to consider myself under house arrest; a six-footer with a side-arm was assigned to make the point clear. I ditched him in the first dark alley and faded from the scene. A schoolteacher named Brown rented the de Salle villa after the disappearance—but as Brown, I'm not free to move. That's where you enter the picture."

"Come to the point, Felix. What was so important that I had to come nine thousand miles in thirteen hours to hear? Do you know where I was?"

He held up a hand. "I know; Barnett told me you'd spent seven months in Bolivia building a cover as a disgruntled veteran of Colonna's Irregulars. Sorry and all that—"

"Another week and I'd have landed an assignment running a shipment of bootleg surgical spares—"

"The frozen kidneys will have to wait for another time." He showed me a Mephistophelean smile. "What I have is far more fun."

"The suspense is unnerving me. Go ahead and spill it."

"All right. Let's begin with the world situation."

"I'd prefer a more cheerful subject—like cancer."

"We may get to that, too, before this one's over." He hitched himself forward, getting down to business. "For most of the last century, John, the world has been at war. We haven't called it that, of course—nobody's actually used nuclear warheads. These are nothing but 'police actions,' or 'internal power realignments,' like the current rumble here in Algeria—maneuvers with live ammunition. But while the powers are whetting their claws on these tupp'ny-'ap'ny shooting matches, they're looking hard for a weapon that would give one state a decisive advantage. In the meantime—stalemate."

"Well," I said, pushing back my chair, "that was mighty interesting, Felix. Thanks for letting me know—"

He leaned across the table. There was a merry glint in his eye; he looked like a devil planning a barbecue.

"We've found that weapon, John."

I settled back into my chair. "All right, I'm listening."

"Very well: Super Hellbombs are out. The answer lies in the other direction, of course. A crowd of infantrymen killing each other isn't war—it's good, healthful sport—just the ticket for working off those perfectly natural aggressions that might otherwise cause trouble. But what if a division or two of foot soldiers suddenly became irresistible? Impervious to attack, deadly on the offensive? Your cosy little brushfire war would turn into a rout for the unlucky side—and there would go your power-balance, shot all to hell—"

"How much better can hand-weapons get? The Norge Combat Imperial weighs six pounds and fires a hundred armor-piercing rounds per second. It's radar-aimed and dead-accurate—"

"I'm talking about something new, John. We call it PAPA—Power Assisted Personal Armament. What it means is—the Invulnerable Man."

I watched Felix swallow half his drink, put the glass down, and sit back with his fingertips together, waiting for my reaction. I nodded casually.

"That's an old idea," I said carelessly. "I used to follow Batman and Robin myself."

"This isn't a Tri-D drama—it's a coordinated development in bioprosthetics, neurosurgery, and myoelectronics. Picture it, John! Microtronics-engineered sense-boosters, wide-spectrum vision, artificially accelerated reflexes, nerve-energy laser-type weapons, all surgically implanted—plus woven-chromalloy body-mail, alligned-crystal metal caps for finger-bones, shins, rib and skull, servo-boosted helical titanium fiber reinforced musculature—"

"You left out the fast-change long-johns with the big red S on them. You know, I always wondered why Clark Kent never got himself arrested in an alley for indecent exposure."

"I had a hand in its development myself," Felix went on, ignoring me. "And I can tell you it's big. You have no idea—"

"But I'd like to have," I cut in. "Especially an idea of what it is I blew a year's work to hear."

He nodded. "I'm just coming to that. For the past six months I've been here in Tamboula, carrying out a study of battle wounds—data we require in the further development of PAPA. And I've turned up a disquieting fact." He poked a finger at me for emphasis. "The number of men reported 'missing in action' amounts to nearly twenty percent of the total casualties."

"There are always a few reluctant warriors who go over the hill."

"Not in the desert, John. I went on then to take a look at civilian missing-persons figures. The world total is close to the two million mark annually. Naturally, this doesn't include data from China and Red India, where one less mouth to feed is noted with relief, if at all. And the Society of American Morticians and Embalmers reports that *not enough people are being buried . . .*"

"I can tell you where part of them are going," I said. "The black market in human organs."

"Yes." Felix nodded. "Doubtless that nefarious trade accounts for some of the discrepancy, particularly in burial figures. But suppose someone were building up a secret force—and outfitting it with an enemy version of PAPA?"

"You can't hide men in those numbers," I said. "The logistical problems alone—"

"I know; but the men are going somewhere. I want to know where."

"I'm afraid I'm beginning to get the picture."

"You still hold your reserve Army commission, I take it?"

I nodded.

"Good. I have your recall orders in my briefcase. They're perfectly legal; I made them myself. You're a Defense Department observer. I've arranged for you to occupy one of our special rooms at the King Faisal."

"I thought CBI assignments were on a voluntary basis."

Felix raised the white eyebrows. "You *are* volunteering, aren't you?"

"I suppose the fact that I'm here answers that one."

"Of course. Now, there's a battle scheduled soon. I haven't been able to find out just when, but I did procure copies of the Utter Top Secret battle plans for both the Free Algerians and the Imperial Moroccans. Death penalty for possession, of course." He took a newspaper from an inner pocket—a folded copy of the *Belfast Messenger*—and dropped it on the table.

"What am I supposed to do, stand around on a hilltop with a pair of binoculars and watch where the men disappear to?"

Felix smiled. "I have a few gadgets for you to field-test. Find out when that battle's scheduled, and I think you'll be able to take a look at just about whatever you want to."

I took the newspaper. "So I'm back in uniform. I suppose I'd better check in with the UN Monitor General."

"Send a card over; perhaps it'll pass unnoticed in the daily mail. I want you to hold your official contacts to the minimum. Stay clear of the Embassy, the police, and the press corps. Your other instructions are with your orders. You'll find a tight-band communicator with the rest of the equipment; keep in touch with me, John—but don't try to contact me at the villa unless it's absolutely necessary."

"You've made some pretty elaborate arrangements. This sort of thing costs money. Who's footing the bill?"

"Let's just say it comes from a special fund." He finished his drink. "Go on over to the Faisal, get settled, and take a look around. I'll expect a preliminary report in a day or two." He stood, replaced the *tabukuk* on the table, gave me a quick handshake, and was gone.

I picked up the newspaper, leafed through it. There were sheets of flimsy paper folded between the pages. I caught a glimpse of tiny print, terrain diagrams, the words Utter Top Secret. I folded it and took the last swallow of my gin. I dropped a five cee note on the table, tucked the paper under my arm, and tried to look casual as I went outside to hail a cab.

The King Faisal Hotel was a two-hundred-story specimen of government-financed construction straight out of Hollywood and the Arabian Nights, turned slummy by five years of North African sun and no maintenance. I paid off my helicab in the shade of thirty yards of cracked glass marquee, managed my own bags through a mixed crowd of shiny-suited officials, Algerian and Moroccan officers mingling quite peaceably outside business hours, beggars in colorful costumes featuring wristwatches and tennis shoes, Arab guides in traditional white lapel-suits, hot-looking tourists, journalists with coffee hangovers, and stolid-faced UN police in short pants with hardwood billies.

I went up the wide steps, past potted yuccas and a uniformed Berber doorman with a bad eye that bored into me like a hot poker. I crossed the lobby to the registration console, slapped the counter, and announced my arrival in tones calculated to dispel any appearance of shyness. A splay-footed Congolese bellhop sidled up to listen as I produced the teleprinted confirmation of my reservation that Felix had supplied. I asked for and received verbal assurances that the water was potable, and was directed to a suite on the forty-fifth level.

It was a pleasant enough apartment. There was a spacious sitting room with old-fashioned aluminum and teak-veneer furniture, a polished composition floor, and framed post-neo-surrealist paintings. Adjoining was a carpeted bedroom with a four-foot tri-D screen, a wide closet, and a window opening onto a view of irregular brickwork across a twelve-foot alley.

Behind the flowered wallpaper, there were other facilities, unknown to the present management—installed, during construction, at the insistence of one of the more secret agencies of the now defunct South African Federation. According to the long, chatty briefing papers Felix had tucked into the newspaper, the CBI had inherited the installation from a former tenant, in return for a set of unregistered fingerprints and a getaway stake.

I looked the room over and spotted a spy-eye in a drawer knob, a microphone among the artificial flowers—standard equipment at the Faisal, no doubt. I would have to make my first order of business a thorough examination of everything . . . as soon as I had a cold shower. I turned to the bedroom—and stopped dead. My right hand made a tentative move toward my gun, and from the shadows a soft voice said, "Uh-uh."

He came through the sitting-room door with a gun in his hand—a middle-sized, neatly dressed man with wispy hair receding from a freckled forehead. He had quick eyes. An inch of clean, white cuff showed at his wrist.

"I was supposed to be gone when you got here," he said quietly. "The boys downstairs slipped up."

"Sure," I said. "They slipped up—and I'm dancing tonight with the *Ballet Russe*." I looked at the gun. "What was I supposed to do, fall down and cry when I saw that?"

His ears turned pink. "It was merely a precaution in the event you panicked." He pocketed the gun, flipped back a lapel to flash some sort of badge. "UN Police," he stated, as though I had asked. "Regulations require all military observers to report to UN Headquarters on arrival—as I'm sure you're aware. You're to come along with me, Mr. Bravais. General Julius wants to interview you personally."

"When did the UN start hiring gun-punks?"

He looked angry. "You can't make me mad, Mr. Bravais."

"I could try. You don't shoot anybody without orders from the boss, do you?" I advanced on him, giving him the kind of grin tri-D villains practice in front of a mirror.

"I could make an exception." His nostrils were white.

"Oh, to hell with it," I said in a careless tone, relaxing. "How about a drink?"

He hesitated. "All right, Mr. Bravais. You understand that there's . . . nothing personal in this."

"I guess you've got a job to do like the rest of us. You're pretty good with that holding-the-breath bit." I grinned happily, demonstrating that I was satisfied, now that I'd shown the opposition that I was nobody's dummy.

"I planned to see the General this afternoon anyway," I said. We had a short one and left together.

Brigadier General Julius was a vigorous-looking, square-jawed, blond-crew-cut type, with an almost unbelievably smooth complexion that might have

earned him the nickname Baby-face, if two fierce,
coal-black eyes hadn't dominated the composition.
The gray UN uniform he wore had been tailored
by an artist, and the three rows of service ribbons
on his chest indicated that, in spite of his youthful
appearance, he had been at the scene of most of
the shooting wars of the past twenty years.

He was wearing the old-fashioned Sam Browne
belt and engineers' boots that the UN High Command liked to affect, but the hand-gun protruding
from the holster at his hip wasn't a pearl-handled
six-shooter; it was the latest thing in pulse-energy
weapons, stark and ugly, meant for murder, not
show.

"American Defense Department, eh?" He glanced
at the copy of the orders Felix had managed for
me, laid them to one side on the bare, highly
polished desk-top. He looked me over thoughtfully.
It was quiet in the office. Faraway, a voice spoke
sing-song Arabic. A fly buzzed at a window.

"I just arrived this afternoon, General," I offered. "I took a room at the King Faisal—"

"Room 4567," Julius said sharply. "You were
aboard BWA flight 87. I'm aware of your movements, Mr. Bravais. As UN Monitor General, I make
it my business to keep informed of everything that
occurs within my command." He had a flat, unpleasant voice, at variance with the wholesome,
nationally-advertised look of him.

I nodded, looking impressed. I thought about
the death penalty attached to the papers in my
pocket, and wondered how much more he knew.
"By golly, that's remarkable, General."

He narrowed his eyes. I had to be careful not to
overdo the act, I reminded myself.

"Makes a man wonder how you can find time
for your other duties," I added, letting a small
gleam of insolence temper the bland smile I was
showing him.

His eyes narrowed even further; I had the feeling that if he squeezed any harder, they would pop out like watermelon seeds.

"I manage, Mr. Bravais," he said, holding his voice smooth. "Just how long can we expect your visit to last?"

"Oh, I wouldn't call it a visit, General. I'm here on PCS, an indefinite tour."

"In that case, I hope you find Tamboula to your liking. You've come at a fortunate time of year. The racing is starting next week, and of course our grouse season is in full swing."

"I've heard a great deal about the ecological projects here," I said. "Quite remarkable to see woodlands springing up from the desert. But I'm afraid I'll have little time to devote to sports. My particular interest is close-support infantry tactics."

"Mr. Bravais." Julius raised a hand. "The feeling seems to have gained wide currency in some quarters that conflicts such as the present one are spectacles carried out for the diversion of the curious. Such is far from the case. A political question is being resolved on the battlefield. UN control will, we trust, limit the scope of the hostilities. Undue attention by representatives of major powers is not likely to assist in that effort. I suggest you consult the official History—"

"I believe the principle of the right of observation has been too well established to require any assertion by me," I stated.

"That is a matter quite outside my cognizance," the General broke in. "My responsibility is to insure that the provisions of the Manhattan Convention are adhered to. You'll understand that the presence of outsiders in the theater unduly complicates that task." He spoke with a curious, flat intensity, watching me with an unwinking gaze, like a gunfighter waiting for the signal to go for his hip.

"General, I'm an accredited official observer; I hope you don't intend to deny me access to my subject?"

"Just what is it you wish to observe?"

"Action—at close range."

Julius shook his head. "That will not be possible tonight—" He stopped abruptly. I permitted myself the liberty of a grin.

"Tonight, eh?"

Julius leaned toward me. He was holding his temper pretty well, but a glint of red fire showed in his eyes.

"You will not approach closer than five miles to the line of action," he said distinctly. "You will report to my adjutant daily at oh-eight hundred hours and submit a schedule of your proposed movements. You will observe a nine o'clock curfew—"

I got to my feet. "You've made a point of calling me 'mister'; if your intelligence apparatus is as good as you say, you're aware that I handle the rank of Brigadier. I haven't asked for any courtesies, and I damned sure haven't gotten any, but don't bother planning my day for me—and don't send out any more gun-handlers. I'll be on my way now, General. Just consider this a courtesy call; I'll operate on my own from now on."

He came around the desk, strode to the door, wrenched it open, turned to face me.

"General Bravais, I cannot be responsible for your safety if you disregard my orders." His voice had the grate of torn steel. I wondered what he'd do if he got just a little madder . . .

"You're not responsible for me in any event, Julius," I snapped. "I suggest you get back to your desk and cook up another chapter of that warmed-over, predigested, salt-free History of yours—"

He was standing rigidly, holding the glass door-knob in a firm clutch. He stiffened as I spoke, then jerked his hand away from the knob; his lip was raised, showing a row of even white teeth.

"I'm not accustomed to insolence in my own headquarters," he grated.

I glanced down at the doorknob. The clear glass was shot through with a pattern of fracture planes.

"I guess you squeezed it too hard, General," I said. He didn't answer. I went on down the narrow, gray-painted corridor and out into the hard, white, North African sunshine.

Chapter Two

I walked half a block at a pace just a trifle faster than the main flow. Then I re-crossed the street, slowed, and gave half a dozen grimy windows filled with moth-riddled mats and hammered brass atrocities more attention than they deserved. By the time I reached the end of the long block, I was sure: the little man with the formerly white suit and the pendulous lower lip was following me.

I moved along, doing enough dodging around vegetable carts and portable *Jimii* shrines to make him earn his salary. He was a clumsy technician, and working alone. That meant that it was a routine shadowing job; Julius didn't consider me to be of any special interest.

At an intersection ahead, a sidewalk juggler had collected a cluster of spectators. I put on a burst, slid through the fringe of the crowd and around the corner. I stopped, counted to ten slowly, then plunged back the way I had come, just in time to collide with my pursuer, coming up fast.

We both yelped, staggered, groped for support, disengaged, muttering excuses, and separated hurriedly. I crossed the street, did an elementary double-back through an arcade, and watched him hurry past. Then I hailed a noisily cruising helicab that had probably been condemned and sold by the City of New York Transit Authority a dozen years earlier.

I caught a glimpse of him standing on the corner looking around worriedly as we lifted off over the rooftops. I didn't waste any sympathy on him; he had been carrying a heavy solid-slug pistol under one arm, a light energy gun under the other, and at least three hypo-spray syringes under his left lapel—probably containing enough assorted poisons to suit any personality he might take a dislike to.

I took out his wallet and riffled through it; there were a couple of hundred Algerian francs, a new two cee American bill, a folded paper containing a white powder, a soiled card imprinted with the name of a firm specializing in unusual photographs, one of the photographs, a week-old horoscope, and a scrap of paper with my name scrawled on it. I didn't know whether it was Julius' handwriting or not, but there was enough of a UN watermark showing to make the question academic.

The cab dropped me in the wide plaza in front of the down-at-heels aluminum and glass Army-Navy-Air Club. I gave the driver the little man's two hundred francs. He accepted it without comment; maybe New York had thrown him in on the deal with the heli.

I had an hour or two to kill. It would be necessary to stay away from my room long enough to give Julius—or anyone else with an interest in my movements—adequate time to look over the evidence planted there to satisfy himself about my mission in Tamboula.

Meanwhile, food was in order. I dodged the outstretched palm of a legless fellow mounted on a wheeled board, and pushed into the cool, pastel-tinted interior of the club, where chattered conversations competed with the background throb of canned music.

In the split-level dining room, I found a table by a sunny window. I had a surprisingly good lunch, lingered over a half-bottle of Château Lascombe '19, and watched the officers of the opposing armies scheduled to go into combat an hour after sundown. They shared tables, chatting and laughing over the brandy and cigars. The bright green of the Free Algerian uniform made a handsome contrast with the scarlet of the Imperial Moroccans.

It was either a civilized way to wage war or a hell of an idiotic way for grown men to behave—I wasn't sure which. I turned my attention from them and devoted the next hour to a careful study of Felix's instructions.

Sunset was beginning to color the sky when I left the club and walked the four blocks to the King Faisal. Just opposite the marquee, a uniformed chauffeur seemed to be having turbine trouble. He stood peering under the raised hood with a worried expression. I went past him and a pair of shady-businessman types, who started a vigorous conversation as I came up, fell silent as I went through the door.

Inside, a slight, colorless European in a tan suit was leaning against the end of the lobby news kiosk. He gave me a once-over that was as subtle as a left hook.

At the desk, the tubby, Frenchified little Arab day manager rolled his eyes toward the far end of the counter. I eased along, made a show of looking through the free tour maps.

He sidled over, perspiring heavily. "M'sieu'—I have to tell you—a man was interrupted searching your room this afternoon." His voice was a damp whisper, like something bubbling up through mud. His breath did nothing to lessen the similarity.

"Sure," I said, angling myself so that the nearest operative could hear me without straining. "But how about the Casbah?"

The manager blinked, then got into the spirit of the thing. "I would have held him for the police, but he made a break for it—"

"Say, that's fine. I've always wanted to see those dancing girls. It is true about the raisin in their belly-button?"

"That fellow—" The manager's eyes rolled toward a tall, thin man who was standing nearby, leafing through a picto-news that looked as though his lunch had been wrapped in it. "He has been here all the afternoon." His voice dropped still more. "I don't like his looks."

I nodded. "You're right," I said loudly. "And he's not even reading; his lips aren't moving."

The newspaper jerked as though he'd just found his name in the obituaries. I went past him to the elevator, waited until the man in the tan suit had followed me in and got settled; then I stepped back off. He hesitated for a moment, then showed me an expression like a man who has just remembered something, and hurriedly got off. I promptly got back on, turned, and gave him a nice smile that he failed to return as the doors closed.

Riding up, I did a little rapid thinking. The clowns in the lobby were a trifle too good to be true; the manager's little contribution was part of the performance, just in case I failed to spot them. Julius wanted to be sure I knew his eye was on me.

I punched a button, got off a floor below my own, and went along to the fire stairs. Palming the little 4mm Browning dart gun Severance had given me, I pushed through the glass door, and went up past a landing littered with used ampoules and the violet-tinted butts of dope-sticks. I came out in the shadows at the end of a poorly-lighted corridor.

My room was halfway along on the left. I put my finger-ring microphone against the door, placed my ear against the ring. I heard the clack of water dripping in the bathroom, the hollow hum of the ventilator, sounds from beyond the windows— nothing else.

I keyed the door quietly and went in; the room was empty, silent, sad in the early-evening light. The key to my briefcase lay where I had left it. I shone my UV pen-light on it, examined the wards; the fluorescent film with which I had coated the web was scored.

That meant that by now Julius was scanning copies of a number of carefully prepared letters and notes establishing my anti-UN, anti-Julius sentiments. It was risky secondary cover to use with a man as sensitive of personal status as the General, but Felix had decided on it after a close study of his dossier. Give a man what he expects to find, and he's satisfied; at least, that was the theory.

For half an hour I puttered, putting away shirts, arranging papers, mixing another drink. At the end of that time I had completed my inspection and was satisfied that nothing new had been installed in the suite since I had seen it a few hours earlier. The IR eye still peered at me from the center knob on the chest of drawers, and the pinhead microphone in the plastic flower arrangement was still in place. I hung a soiled undershirt over the former; the audio pickup didn't bother me. I'd just make it a point to move quietly.

It was almost dark now—time to be going. I made a few final noises in the bathroom with running water and clattering toilet articles; then I flipped off the lights, made the bed creak as I stretched out on it, then rose carefully, entered the closet, and soundlessly shut the door.

Following Felix's written instructions, I unscrewed the old-fashioned fluorescent tube from the ceiling fixture, pressed the switch concealed in the socket; the hatch in the end wall rolled smoothly back. I stepped through, closed it behind me, went along a narrow passage that ended in an iron ladder leading up.

At the top, I cracked my head in the dark. I felt for the latch, lifted the panel, and pulled myself up into the stifling heat of the dark, cramped room Severance had fitted out as my forward command post. It wasn't much to look at—a seven-by-twelve-foot space, low-ceilinged, blank-walled, with a grimy double-hung window at one end giving a view of irregular black rooftops, and, far away, tall palms like giant dandelions against a sky of luminous deep blue.

I closed the shutters and switched on the ceiling light. A steel locker against the wall opened to the combination Severance had given me; if I had made an error, a magnesium flare would have reduced the contents to white-hot ash.

I pulled the door wide, took out a limp, fish-scale-textured coverall with heavy fittings molded into the fabric at the small of the back and the ankles. I pulled off my jacket, struggled into the garment. It was an optical-effect suit—one of the CBI's best-kept secrets. It had the unusual property of absorbing some wave lengths of light and re-emitting them in the infra-red, reflecting others in controlled refraction patterns. It was auto-tuned over the entire visible spectrum, and was capable of duplicating any background pattern short of a clan Ginsberg tartan. I couldn't walk down *le Grand Cours* in Paris in it without causing a few puzzled stares, but in any less crowded setting it was as close an approximation of a cloak of invisibility as science had come up with. It was the Cover Lab's newest toy, and was worth a hundred thousand cees in small, unmarked bills in any of the secret marketplaces of the world.

The second item I would need was a compact apparatus the size and shape of an old-style cavalry canteen, fitted with high-velocity gas jets and heavy clips that locked to matching fittings on the suit. I lifted it—it was surprisingly heavy—and clamped it in place against my chest. Broad woven-wire straps stitched into the suit took up the weight. I tried the control—a two-inch knob at the center of the unit.

Immediately I felt the slightly nauseous sensation of free-fall. The surface of the suit crackled softly as static charges built and neutralized themselves against the field-interface. Then my toes were reaching for the floor. My focused-phase field generator was in working order.

I switched it off, and gravity settled over me again like a lead cape. I checked the deep thigh-pockets of the suit; there was a pair of three-ounce, hundred-power binocular goggles, a spring-steel sheath knife, a command-monitor communicator tunable to the frequencies of both combatants as well as the special band available only to Felix. I pressed the *send* button, got no reply. Felix was out.

In a buttoned-down pocket, I found a 2mm needler, smaller and lighter than the standard Navy model I normally carried. Its darts were charged with a newly developed venom guaranteed to kill a charging elephant within a microsecond of contact. I tucked it back in its fitted holster with the same respect a snakehandler gives a krait.

I was hot in the suit. Sweat was already beginning to trickle down my back. I switched off the lights, opened the shutters and the window, crawled through and found a precarious foothold on a ledge.

The air was cooler here. I took a couple of deep

breaths to steady my nerves, carefully not looking down the sheer five-hundred-foot face of the building. I groped the communicator from my pocket, made another try to raise Felix. Still nothing. I would have to move without the reassurance of knowing that someone was available to record my last words.

I twisted the lift control. At once, the close, airless pressure of the field shut away the faint breeze. Tiny blue sparks arced to the wall at my back. I was lifting now, feeling the secure pressure against my feet drifting away. I pushed clear, twisting myself to a semihorizontal chest-down position, and waved my arms, striving for equilibrium, fighting against the feeling that in another instant I would plummet to the pavement. It was a long way down, and although my intellect told me my flying carpet would support up to a half-ton of dead weight, my emotions told me I was a foolish and extremely fragile man.

I touched the jet control lever, and at the forward surge, my vertigo left me; suddenly I was a swift, soundless bird, sweeping through the wide night sky on mighty pinions—

A dark shape loomed in front of me; I gave the field-strength knob a convulsive twist, cleared an unlighted roof antenna by a foot. From now on, I told myself, it would be a good idea to do my pinion-sweeping with a little more caution. I slowed my forward motion and angled steeply up.

The lights were dwindling away below—the glitter of *l'Avenue Organisation des Nations Unis*, the hard shine from the windows of hotels and office buildings. The sounds that floated up to me were dull, muted by the field. At an estimated five-hundred-foot altitude, I took a bearing on the blue beacon atop the control tower at Hammarskjöld Field, a mile east of the town. I opened my jets to full bore and headed for the battlefield.

Chapter Three

I hung three hundred feet above the sparsely wooded hilltop where the blue-clad Moroccans had set up their forward field HQ. I was jiggling my position controls to counter a brisk breeze, and mentally calculating the odds against my being bagged by a wild shot. With my goggles turned to low mag and IR filter, I was able to make out a cluster of officers around a chart table, three recon cars parked behind the crest of the hill with their drivers beside them, and a line of dug-in riflemen on the forward slope. Five miles to the north, the pale blue flashes of the Algerians' opening bombardment winked against the horizon.

The battle's objective was a bombed-out oasis occupying the center of the shallow valley ringed by the low hills over one of which I now hovered. According to Felix's Utter Top Secret Battle Plan, the Algerians would thrust their right forward in a feint to the Moroccan left, while quickly bringing up the bulk of their light armor behind the screen of the hills on the enemy right. The Moroccan strategy was to sit tight in defensive entrenchments until the enemy intention became clear, then launch a drive straight down the valley, with a second column poised to take the Algerians in the flank as soon as they struck from cover at the Moroccan flank. It seemed like a nice, conventional exercise, and I felt sure the boys would enjoy it a lot.

The Algerian ballistic shells were making vivid puffs high above the valley now, followed by laggard thumps of sound, as the Moroccan antiballistic artillery made their interceptions. At each flash, the details of the battlefield below blinked into momentary clarity; it was an almost steady flickering, like heat lightning on a summer evening.

I turned up my binocular magnification, scanned the distant Algerian massing area for signs of their main column moving out. They were a minute or two ahead of schedule. The churn of dust was just beginning to rise above the lead element; then antidust equipment went into operation and the cloud dissipated. Now I could pick out the tiny pinpoints of running lights, coming swiftly around in the shelter of the distant hills to form the arrowhead of the Algerian attack.

I lifted myself another hundred feet, jetted toward their route of advance. They were coming up fast—risking accidents in the dark—to beat the best time the Moroccans would have estimated was possible. I arrived over the cut through which they would turn to make their dash for the oasis, just as the lead tank rounded into it—a massive Bolo Mark II, now running without lights. The Moroccans, caught in the trap of overconfidence in their intelligence analysis, still showed no signs of recognizing the danger. The first squad of four Algerian combat units was through the pass, gunning out into the open.

Belatedly now, a volley of flares went up from the Moroccan side; the tanks had been spotted. Abruptly the valley burned dead-white under a glare like six small suns; each racing tank was the base of a cluster of long, bounding shadows of absolute black.

I dropped lower, watched the second and third elements follow the lead units through the pass. The fourth unit of the last squad, lagging far behind, slowed, came to a stop. A minute passed; then he started up, moving slowly ahead, bypassing the designated route of march.

Out on the plain, Moroccan tanks were roaring out from their positions two miles to my left, guns stabbing across the plain, both columns together in a hammerblow at the Algerian surprise thrust. Below me, the lone tank trundled heavily away from the scene of action, veering to the left now, moving into broken ground. The approved Battle Plan had included no detachment operating independently on the Algerian left; if the wandering Bolo were detected by the monitors—as it must inevitably be within minutes—the battle was forfeit, the fury and destruction all for nothing. Something was up:

I ignored the battle on the plain. I dropped to a hundred feet, followed the tank as it lumbered down a shale-littered slope into deep darkness.

I moved carefully between towering walls of shattered rock, fifty feet above the floor of the dry wadi along which the Bolo moved in a sluggish crawl. A finger of light from its turret probed uncertainly ahead as though exploring new and dangerous territory. It negotiated an awkward turn, halted. I saw a faint gleam as its hatch cycled; then a silhouetted man clambered out, dropped to the ground; the tank sat with turbines idling, its searchlight fixed aimlessly on a patch of bare rock, like the gaze of a dead man.

I turned up the sensitivity of my goggles, tried to penetrate the darkness. I couldn't see the driver. I moved closer—

Something massive and dark was coming up the ravine toward me, hovering two yards above the ground. It was a flattish shape, roughly oval, dull-colored, casting a faint blue-green glow against the rocky walls as it maneuvered gently around a projecting buttress, settled in close to the Bolo.

For a moment nothing more happened. The idling engine of the tank was a soft growl against stillness, punctuated by the sounds of distant battle. Then there was a heavy thud. The sound reminded me of a steer I had seen poleaxed once in a marketplace in Havana . . .

I worked my binocular controls, tuning well over into the IR. The scene before me took on a faint, eerie glow. I maneuvered to the right, made out an oblong path of lesser blackness against the ground.

Abruptly, shadows were sliding up the rock wall. The angry snarl of an engine sounded from behind me. I lifted quickly, moved back against the ravine face. The armored shape of a late-model command car careened into view, an opaque caterpillar of dust boiling up behind it. The blue-white lance of its headlight scoured the canyon floor, picked up the dusty side of the tank, reflecting from the rim of its open hatch. The car slowed, stopped directly below me, hovering on its air-cushion, the blue-black muzzles of its twin infinite repeaters poking through the armor-glass canopy, centered on the tank.

A minute passed; faint, flickering light stuttered against the sky in the direction of the battle. The car below sank, came to rest slightly canted on the boulder-strewn ground. Its engines died. Metal clanked as the door slid open. A man in a dull-green Algerian field uniform stepped out, a pistol in his hand. He shouted in Arabic. There was no reply.

He walked forward into the settling dust in the alley of light from the car's headlamp, his shadow stalking ahead. I saw the glint of the palm-leaf insignia on his shoulder; a major, probably the squadron commander—

He stopped, seemed to totter for a moment, then fell stiffly forward. He hit hard on his face, and lay without moving. I hung where I was, absolutely still, waiting.

From the darkness beyond the stalled tank, a creature came into view, padding silently on broad, dead white paws like ghastly caricatures of human hands. Stiff, coarse hair bristled on the lean, six-foot body, growing low on the forehead of a naked face like a fanged and snouted skull. A pattern of straps crisscrossed the razor back; light winked from metal fittings on the harness.

It came up to the man who lay face-down with his feet toward me, fifty feet below. It settled itself on its haunches, fumbled with its obscenely human hands in a pouch at its side. I caught a glint of light from polished instruments; then it crouched over the man, set to work.

I heard a grating sound, realized that I had been grinding my teeth together in a rictus of shock. Cold sweat trickled down the side of my neck under the suit.

Down below, the creature worked busily, its gaunt, narrow-shouldered body screening its task. It shifted position, presenting its back now, the long curve of its horse-like neck.

I had to force my hand to move. I slipped the dartgun from its fitted pocket, flipped off the safety. The beast labored on, absorbed in its victim. Quick motions of its elbows reflected its deft manipulations.

A feeling of nightmarish unreality seemed to hang over the scene: the wink and rumble of the artillery beyond the hills, the knife-like sharpness of the shadows thrown by the light of the command car, the intent, demonic figure. I took careful aim just below a triangular clasp securing two straps that crossed the arched back, and fired.

The creature twitched a patch of hide impatiently, went on with its work. I aimed again, then lowered the gun without firing a second time; if one jolt of Felix's venom had no effect, two wouldn't help. I flattened myself in the pocket of shadow against the cliff-face, watched as the alien rose to a grotesque two-legged stance, then pranced away on its rear hands toward the body of the driver, lying crumpled beside the Bolo.

The major lay on his back now, the cap nearby, his gun a yard away. There was blood on his face and on the dusty stone under him. I estimated the distance to the command car, gauging the possibility of reaching it and training the forward battery on the monstrosity now leaning over the second man—

There was a sudden, sharp yelp. The alien darted a few steps, collided glancingly with the massive skirt of the Bolo, veered toward me. I caught a glimpse of a gaping mouth, a ragged, black tongue, teeth like needles of yellow bone.

The stricken demon bit at its rear quarters, running in a tight circle like a dog chasing its tail, yelping sharply; then it was down, kicking, scrabbling with its pale, flat hands, raising a roil of dust. Then it stiffened and lay still.

I dropped quickly to the ground, switched off the lift-field. I caught the reek of exhaust fumes, the hot-stone odor of the desert, and a sharp, sour smell that I knew came from the dead creature.

I went to the body of the major and bent over it. The face was slack, the eyelids unnaturally sunken.

There was a clean wound across the forehead at the hairline. The hair was matted with glistening blood.

I turned him on his face. The top of his skull had been cut free; it hung in place on a hinge of scalp. Inside the glistening red-black cavity was—nothing.

I leaned closer. A deep incision gaped from the base of the skull down under the collar. Very little blood had leaked from it; the heart had stopped before the wound was made.

The alien lay fifteen feet away. I looked across at it, my breathing coming fast and shallow, hissing between teeth that were bared in a snarl. Every instinct I owned was telling me to put space between myself and the demonic creature that had walked like a beast but had used its hands like a man.

I had heard of hackles rising; now I felt them. I gripped the gun tighter as I crossed the last few feet, stood looking down at the sparse, rumpled coat through which dull gray-pink skin showed. I prodded the body with a boot; it was stiff, inert, abnormally heavy. I pushed harder, rolled it over. At close range, the face was yellowish white, dry, porous-textured. The hands were outflung, palms up, bloody from the trepanning of the major; near one lay a bulging, gallon-sized sack, opaque with dust.

I stepped around to it, knelt and wiped a finger across the bulge of the surface; it was yielding, warm to the touch. Pinkish fluid wobbled under the taut membrane.

I brushed away more dust. Now I could see a pink, jelly-like mass suspended in the liquid. It had a furrowed surface, like sun-baked mud, and from its underside hung a thick, curled stem, neatly snipped off three inches down.

I prodded the bag. The mass stirred; a snow-white sphere just smaller than a golf ball wavered into view, turning to show me a ring of amber-brown with a black center dot.

The battle sounds were slackening now. It wouldn't be long before another vehicle came along the ravine in search of the missing Bolo and the officer who had followed it. I stood, feeling my heart pound as though I had run a mile, fighting down the sickish feeling that knotted my stomach. I didn't have much time, and there were things to be done—now.

The tankman, lying awkwardly beside his massive machine, was dead, already cooling to the touch. I went back to the fallen demon, went through the pouches attached to the creature's harness, and found a case fitted with scalpels, forceps, a tiny saber saw. There was a supply of plastic containers and a miniature apparatus with attached tubing—probably a pump-and-filter combination for drawing off plasma. There was another container, packed with ampoules of a design I had seen recently—on the landing in my hotel. The thought was like a cold finger on my spine.

The last pouch yielded a scrap of smooth, tough paper, imprinted with lines of pot-hooks of a sort I had never seen before. I tucked it away in my knee-pocket, got to my feet. The paper was better than nothing as evidence that I hadn't been the dreamer of a particularly horrible nightmare. But I needed something more compelling—something that would communicate some of the shock I felt. Felix needed to see that skull-white face . . .

The ravine was still quiet; maybe I had time.

I ran to the car, started it up and brought it forward, halted it beside the dead man. I jumped down and lifted the limp body into the cockpit. I remounted, maneuvered up beside the dead alien. I opened the cargo compartment at the rear of the car, then gritted my teeth and grasped the crea-

ture's hind wrists. Through the gloved hands of
the suit, the bristles were as stiff as scrub-brushes.

I dragged the corpse to the car, used the power
of the suit to lift the three-hundred-pound weight,
and tumbled it inside.

I went back for the sack containing the brain,
put it on the seat beside the dead major, them
climbed in and headed back up the ravine. As I
reached the first turn, a glare of light projected the
car's moving shadow on the rock wall ahead. I
turned, saw a brilliant flare fountain from the open
hatch of the Bolo.

I gunned the car, and felt a tremor run through
the rock an instant before I heard the blast. Small
stones rained down, bounded off the canopy and
hood. Either the tank had been mined for automatic destruction if abandoned or else the creature I had killed had set a time-charge to eliminate
the traces of his visit.

I tramped on the throttle, holding my thoughts
rigidly on my driving. I wasn't ready yet to think
about the implications of what I had seen. I could
feel the full shock of it, lurking in the wings, waiting to jump out and send me screaming for a
policeman—but that would have to wait. Now, I
was concerned only with getting clear with my
prize while there was still time.

Because there was no doubt that in a little
while—when whoever, or whatever, was awaiting
the return of the brain-thief realized that something was awry—a variety of hell would break
loose that would make ordinary death and destruction seem as mild and wholesome as a spring
morning.

I skirted the hills where floodlights were glaring
now in the Moroccan camp. The cease-fire had
apparently been sounded; UN monitors would be
moving out on the field, tallying casualties, look-

ing for evidence of illegal weapons, checking out complaints by both sides of Battle Plan violations. I hoped that in the general excitement the absence of the command car would go unnoticed for now. The road into Tamboula was a wide, well-patrolled highway. I avoided it, took a route across a wasteland of stunted mesquite. I skirted a trenched and irrigated field, orderly in the light of the new-risen moon, then stopped by a clump of trees fifty yards from Felix's villa, a former farmhouse, converted by the CBI into an armored fortress capable of withstanding a siege that would have leveled Stalingrad. The windows were dark. I took out my communicator, pressed the red button that tuned it to Felix's special equipment.

"Wolfhound here, Talisman. Anybody home?"

There was no reply. I tried again; still nothing. It was too early to start worrying, but I started anyway. There were sounds on the road behind me now, the surviving troops, who—tired and happy after their evening's fun—were starting back to their billets in town. Even if my borrowed car hadn't been missed yet, the sight of it would inspire laggard memories. I couldn't stay here.

General Julius had been less than enthusiastic about my presence in Tamboula; my arrival at his headquarters in a stolen Algerian command car would hardly be calculated to soothe him. But even a stuffed shirt of a political appointee would have a hard time shrugging off what I had to show him. I gunned the car around the side of the house, cut across a field of cabbages, mounted the raised highway, and barreled for the city at flank speed.

Chapter Four

I parked the car beside a gleaming Monojag in the well-lighted but deserted ten-car garage under UN headquarters. I pulled off the suit and harness, took the lift to the third floor, walked through deserted offices to General Julius' door, and went in without knocking. He was there, sitting at his desk, square-shouldered and grim-jawed, like a cornered police chief promising the press an arrest at any moment. He didn't move as I came up.

"I'm glad I caught you, General," I said. "Something's happened that you should know about."

He was a long time reacting to my presence—as though he were a long way off. His eyes seemed to focus slowly. His mouth opened, then closed hard.

"Yes?" he snapped. "What do you want?"

"Have you had a report of a missing Bolo—and a command car?"

His dead-black eyes narrowed. I had his attention now. The room seemed very still. "Missing combat units?" Julius said expressionlessly. "Go on."

"An Algerian Mark II wandered off the beaten path. It wound up in a ravine about three miles south of the action."

Julius stared at me. "You observed this?" His fingers squeaked on the desk-top.

"That's right. The car followed the Bolo in. A major was driving it—"

"You imply that this vehicle maneuvered in violation of the Battle Plan?"

"They left the field of action and went south. Let's not play footsie about the Battle Plan. Sure I had a copy. Grow up, General; I'm not a reporter for a family magazine—I'm here on business. Part of my business is to know what's going on."

"My orders to you—"

"Don't ride a busted bluff down in flames, General. How about that Bolo?"

Julius leaned forward. "A ravine, south of the battleground?"

"That's right. There's not much left of it; it blew—"

"How close were you?"

"Close enough."

"And the car?"

"It's downstairs, in your garage."

"You brought it here?"

I let that one ride. Julius cocked his head, as though listening to voices I couldn't hear.

"Where did you find the vehicle?" he asked finally.

"Where the driver left it."

"And you took it?"

"Look, General, I didn't come here to talk about traffic violations. I saw something out there—"

"You deliberately disobeyed me?" Julius' classically chiseled upper lip was writhing back in a snarl; behind his eyes red fires burned. It seemed to be taking all his will power not to bite me. "You entered the battle zone—"

"Forget that. There's some kind of vehicle sitting out there near what's left of the Bolo. The blast probably caught it, but there should be enough to work on. I saw what got out of it. It wasn't human. It killed the driver and the major . . ." I stopped talking then, belatedly. What I was saying sounded wild, even to me. "Come with me, General," I said. "I'll show you."

Abruptly, he laughed—a harsh, tinny sound.

"I see . . . it's a joke," he said. He got to his feet. "Just one moment. I have an important call to make." I stared after him as he strode across the room, disappeared into an inner office.

There was a call-screen beside his desk. I went to it, cautiously eased the conference switch to the *on* position. There was a soft hum, nothing more. A pad lay on top of the cabinet, marks scribbled on it. I half turned away—

I stood looking down at the paper, my heart starting to thump again under my ribs. The lines on the paper were not mere random jottings; they were letters, words; words in an alien script. I had seen similar pot-hooks less than an hour before—on the paper I had taken from the pocket of the demon.

At that moment, Julius strode back into the room, his face fixed in a smile as authentic as the gold medals on a bottle of vermouth.

"Now, General Bravais," he said in a tone of forced geniality, "why don't you and I sit down and have a quiet drink together . . ."

I shook my head. It was time for me to stop talking and start thinking—something I hadn't done much of since the four-handed horror had stalked out of the shadows and into my world-picture. I had come here babbling out my story, wanting someone to share the shattering thing I had seen—but my choice of confidants had been as poor as the judgment I had been showing ever since I had left the ravine. I had channeled my panic into an outward semblance of sober reasonable action—but it had been panic nonetheless.

Julius had his office booze cabinet open now; shelves with ice-buckets, tongs, bottles, glasses deployed themselves at the touch of a button.

"What about a Scotch, General?" he suggested. "Bourbon? Rye? Irish?"

"I'd better be on my way, General," I said. I moved toward the door. "Perhaps I got a little too excited. Maybe I was seeing things." My hand was feeling for the dart gun—until I realized, with a pang of unpleasant excitement, that I had left it in the car with the lift-suit. . . .

"Of course, you're probably famished. I'll just order up a bite; I haven't eaten myself."

"No, thanks, General. I'm pretty tired. I'll check in at my hotel and . . ."

My voice trailed off foolishly. I—and Felix—had gone to considerable trouble to leave the public with the impression that I was tucked safely away in my room. Now I was here, putting Julius on notice that while his watchdogs were curled happily on my doorstep, I had been out on the town—and the super-secret equipment Felix had lent me was lying unattended in the car.

"I have quarters right here in the building, General Bravais," Julius said. "No need to go back to your room. Just make yourself comfortable here. . ."

I held up a hand, fixed a silly smile in place; it came naturally. I felt as phony as a man who reaches for his wallet after a big dinner and feels nothing but his hipbone.

"I have a couple of appointments this evening," I gushed, "and some papers I want to go over. And I need to get my notes in shape—" I had the door open now. "What about first thing in the morning?"

Julius was coming toward me, with an expression on his face that human features had never been shaped for. A good soldier knows when it's time to run.

I slammed the door on the square, tight-lipped face, sprinted for the lift, then bypassed it, plunged for the stairs. Behind me, there was a heavy crash, the pound of feet. I skidded through the scattered butts on the landing, leaped down five steps at a time. I could hear Julius above, not getting any closer, but not losing any ground, either.

As I ran, I tried to picture the layout of the garage. The lift door had been in the center of the wall, with another door to its left. The car was parked fifteen feet from it; it would be to my left as I emerged . . .

I needed more time. There was a trick for getting downstairs quickly—if my ankles could take it . . .

I whirled around the second landing, half-turned to the left, braced my feet, the left higher than the right, and jumped. My feet struck at an angle, skidded; I shot down as though I were on a ski slope. I slammed the next landing, took a quick step, leaped again.

The door to the garage was in front of me now. I wrenched it open, skidded through, banged it shut. There was a heavy thumb latch. I flipped it, heard the solid *snick!* as it seated. A break; maybe I had time . . .

I dashed for the car, leaped the side—

A thunderous blow struck the heavy metal-clad fire door behind me. I scrambled into the seat, kicked the starter, saw dust whirl from beneath the car. There was a second clangorous shock against the armored door. I twisted, saw it jump, then, unbelievably, bulge—

The metal tore with a screech. A hand groped through the jagged opening, found the latch, plucked it from the door as though it were made of wet paper.

The car was up on its air cushion now; I backed it as the door swung wide. Julius came through, ran straight for me.

I wrenched the wheel over, gunned the twin turbines, the car leaped forward, caught Julius square across the chest with a shock as though I had hit a hundred-year oak. It carried him backward. I saw furrows appear in the chromalloy hood as his fingers clawed—

Then the car thundered against the masonry wall, rebounded in a rain of falling bricks. Through the dust I saw Julius' arm come up, strike down at the crumpled metal before him with a shock that I felt through the frame. There was a howl of metal in agony—then a deafening rattle as the turbines chattered to a halt. The car dropped with a bone-bending jar. I stumbled out half-dazed, and stood staring at General Julius' dust-covered head and shoulders pinned between the ruined car and the wall, one arm outflung, the other plunged through metal into the heart of the engine.

I became aware of voices, turned, and saw a huddle of locals, one or two pale, wide-eyed European faces at the open garage doors. Like a man in a daze, I walked around the rear of the wrecked car, pulled open the door of the Monojag parked beside it, transferred the suit and the lift-harness to the other car.

I took the sheath knife from the suit pocket, went to the cargo compartment of the Turbocar, threw open the lid. A wave of unbelievable stench came from the body of the dead thing inside. I gritted my teeth, sawed at the skin of the long, lean neck. It was like hacking at an oak root. I saw a pointed ear almost buried in the coarse bristles. I grasped it, worked at it with the keen blade. Brownish fluid seeped out as I worried through it. Behind me, the curious spectators were shouting questions back and forth. With a savage slash, I

freed the ear, jammed it in a pocket, then whirled
to the Monojag, jumped in, started up. I backed,
wheeled out, and away down the side street. In the
mirror, I saw the crowd start cautiously forward.

Driving aimlessly along dark streets, I tried again
and failed to raise Felix on my communicator. I
switched on the radio, caught a throaty male con-
tralto muttering a song of strange perversions. On
another channel, wild brass instruments squealed
a hybrid snycopated *alhaza*. On a third, a voice
gushing with synthetic excitement reported the
latest evidence of an imminent cold-war thaw, in
the form of a remark made at a reception by the
wife of an Albanian diplomat in the hearing of the
Chinese chargé, to the effect that only French wine
would be served at a coming dinner in honor of
the birthday of the Cuban President.

The next item was about a madman who had
murdered an Algerian officer. The victim's head-
less body had been found in a stolen military vehicle that had been wrecked and abandoned near
UN headquarters . . .

I looked at my watch. Julius' heirs were fast
workers; it had been exactly sixteen minutes since
I had left his body pinned under the wreckage of
the command car.

Chapter Five

I parked the Turbocar three blocks from the King Faisal, took five minutes to don the OE suit, complete with lift-harness, then drove slowly along toward the hotel. The news bulletin had said nothing about the car I was now in; it had also failed to mention the dead general, the body of the alien, or the bagged brain. It wasn't mere sloppy reporting; the version of the story that was being released had been concocted hurriedly but carefully. I could expect that other measures would have been taken, with equal care. It was no time for me to allow myself the luxury of errors in strategy—but there were things in the secret room I needed.

The hotel was just ahead. I slowed, edged toward the curb. To an observer, the car would appear to be empty, a remote pickup of the type assigned to VIPs who objected to sharing transportation with anything as unreliable as a human driver.

A doorman in an ornate Zouave uniform came

forward, glanced into the car as it came to a stop.
He looked around sharply, turned, and took three
steps to a call-screen, talked tersely into it. Moments later, two hard-eyed men in unornamented
dark coveralls strode from the hotel entry, fanned
out to approach the car from two sides.

I had seen enough to get the general idea. I
nudged the car into motion, steering between the
two wide-shouldered, lean-hipped trouble boys. One
whipped out a three-inch black disc—a police
control-override. A red light blinked on the dash;
the car faltered as the external command came to
brake.

I gunned it hard, felt the accelerator jam. The
nearer man was swinging alongside now, reaching
for the door. An unfamiliar lever caught my eye,
mounted to the left of the cruise control knob; I hit
it, felt the accelerator go to the floor. There was a
sharp tug, a rending of metal, and the car leaped
ahead. In the mirror I saw one of the two men
down, skidding to the curb. The other stood, feet
apart, bringing a handgun to bear.

I cut the wheel, howled into a cross street as
solid slugs sang off the armored bubble next to my
ear. Ahead, a startled man in a white turban leaped
from my path. Late drinkers at a lone lighted sidewalk café stared as I shot past. I got the needler
out, put it on the seat beside me. I half expected to
see a roadblock pop up ahead; if it did, I would hit
it wide open. I had no intention of stopping until I
had put a healthy distance between myself and the
man I had seen in the mirror—scrambling to his
feet, still holding in his hand the door handle he
had torn from the car.

I parked the car a block farther along, on a dark
side street. I palmed the gun, slid out, stood in the
darkness under a royal palm with a trunk like

gray concrete, giving my instincts a chance to whisper warnings.

It was very still here; far away, I heard a worn turbine coming closer, then going away. The moon was up now, an icy blue-white disc glaring in a pale night sky, casting shadows like the memory of a noonday long ago.

My instincts were as silent as everything else. Maybe the beating they'd been taking all evening had given them the impression I didn't need them any more. Maybe they were right; I hadn't slowed down yet long enough to let what I had seen filter through the fine sieve of my intellect; I had been playing it by ear from moment to moment; maybe that was the best technique, when half of what you saw was unbelievable and the other half impossible.

I tried to raise Felix again; no answer. He had warned me to stay clear of police stations; after my reception at UN headquarters, it was easy advice to take. He had also told me to stay clear of his villa—except in emergencies. That meant now. I activated the lift-belt, rose quickly, and headed west.

No lights showed in the villa as I came in on it from the east. I used my nearly depleted jets to brake to a stop against the flow of the river of dark night air. Then I hovered, looking down on the moonlit rooftop of Algerian tile, the neat garden, the silvery fields stretching away to the desert. I took the communicator from the suit pocket, tried again to raise Felix. A sharp vibration answered my signal. I brought the device up close to my face.

"Felix!" I almost shouted, my words loud in my ears inside the muffling field. "Where the hell have you been? I've—" I broke off, suddenly wary.

"John, old boy. Where are you? There's been the

devil to pay!" It was Felix's familiar voice—but I had had a number of expensive lessons in caution since sundown.

"Where are you?"

"I'm at the house; just got in. I tried to check with you at the hotel, but little men with beady eyes seemed to be peering at me from every keyhole. I gave it up and came here. Where've you been these last hours? Something's going on in the town. Nothing to do with you, I hope?"

"I tried to call you," I said, "where were you?"

"Yes—I felt the damned thing buzzing in my pocket; as it happened, it wasn't practical for me to speak just then. When I tried you, I got no reply."

"I've been busy; guess I missed your buzz."

There was a moment's silence. "So you were mixed up in whatever it is that's got them running about like ants in a stirred hill?"

"Maybe. I want to see you. Meet me in town—at the Club."

"Is that safe, John?"

"Never mind. Get started; half an hour." I broke off. Down below, the house was a silent block of moonwhitened masonry; a low-slung sports car squatted by the front door. Foreshortened trees cast ink-black shadows on the gravel drive.

The front door opened, closed quickly. Felix's tall, lean figure came down the steps, reached the car in three strides. He slid into the seat, started up, backed quickly, headed off along the curving way. His lights came on, dimmed.

"All right, that's far enough," I said. "I just wanted to be sure you were there, and alone." Below, the car slowed, pulled to the side of the road. I saw Felix craning his neck, his face a white blob in the pale light.

"It's that serious, eh, John? Right. Shall I go back to the house?"

"Put the car in the drive and get out."

I dropped lower, watching him comply. I gained fifty feet upwind, curved in so that the wind would bring me across the drive. Felix stopped the car by the front door, stepped out, stood, hands in pockets, looking around as though deciding whether it was a nice enough night for a stroll.

I corrected my course, dropped lower; I was ten feet above the dry lawn now, sweeping toward him silently at fifteen miles an hour. His back was toward me. At the last instant, he started to turn— just as my toe caught him behind the ear in a neatly placed kick. He leaped forward, fell headlong, and lay face down, arms outflung. I dropped to the drive, shut down the field, stood with the gun ready in my hand, watching him.

The impact had been about right—not the massive shock of slamming against whatever it was that had masqueraded as General Julius—or the metal-shearing wrench that had torn the door handle from the car.

I walked toward him, knelt cautiously, rolled him over. His mouth was half open, his eyes shut. I took the sheath knife from my knee pouch, jabbed him lightly in the side; the flesh seemed reassuringly tender. I took his limp hand and pricked it. The skin broke; a bead of blood appeared, black in the dim light.

I sheathed the knife with a hand that shook. "Sorry Felix," I muttered. "I had to be sure you weren't machined out of spring steel, like a couple of other people I've met this evening."

Inside, I laid Felix out on a low divan in the dark room, put a cold damp cloth on his forehead, and waved a glass of plum brandy under his nose. There was a bluish swelling behind his ear, but his pulse and respiration were all right. Within a minute he was stirring, making vague, swimming motions, and then suddenly sitting up, eyes open, his hand groping toward his underarm holster.

"It's all right, Felix," I said. "You had a bump on the head, but you're among friends."

"Some friends." He put a hand up, touched the bruise, pronounced a couple of Arabic curses in a soft voice. "What the devil's up, John? I let you out of my sight for an hour or two, and the whole damned official apparatus goes into a Condition Red flap."

"I used the gear. I tracked a Bolo down a side trail, about three miles off the battle map. I saw things—things I'm going to have trouble telling you about."

Felix was looking at me keenly. "Take it easy, old man. You look as though you'd had a bit of a shaking." He got to his feet, wavered for a moment, went across to the bar.

"No lights," I said.

"Who're we hiding out from?" He got out glasses and a bottle, poured, came back and sat down. He raised his glass.

"Confusion to the enemy," he said. I took a sip, then a gulp. The Scotch felt as smooth as cup grease.

"I'll try to take it in order," I said. "I watched the tank stop; the driver got out—and fell on his face."

"No shots, signs of gas, anything of that sort?"

"Nothing. I was fifty feet away, and felt nothing, smelled nothing, saw nothing. Of course the field—"

"Wouldn't stop a gas, or a vibratory, effect. Was there any fluorescing of the field interface?"

I shook my head, went on with my story. Felix listened quietly until I mentioned the poisoned dart I had fired.

His face fell like a bride's cake. "You must have missed."

"After about two minutes, it got the message;

yelped a few times, chased its tail, had a modest fit, and died."

"My God! The thing must have the metabolism of a rock crusher. Two minutes, you say?"

"Yep." I went on with the story. When I finished, he frowned thoughtfully.

"John, are you sure—"

"Hell, I'm not sure of anything. The easiest hypothesis is that I'm out of my mind. In a way, I'd prefer that." I fumbled, brought out the ear I had cut from the dead alien.

"Here, take a look at this and then tell me I sawed it off poor old Bowser, who just wanted me to play with his rubber rat."

Felix took the two-inch triangle of coarse-haired gristle, peered at it in the near-dark. "This is from the thing in the canyon?"

"That's right." I tried another pocket, found the printed hieroglyphics I had taken from the creature's pouch. "And this. Maybe it's a simple Chinese laundry list—or a Turkish recipe for goulash. Maybe I'm having delusions on a grand scale."

Felix stood. "John . . ." He eyed me sharply. "What you've turned up calls for special measures. We can't take chances now—not until we know what it is we're up against. I'm going to let you in on a secret I've sworn to protect with my life."

He led me to a back room, moved a picture, pressed unmarked spots on the wall. A trap slid back in the floor.

"This is the Hole," he said. "Even the CBI doesn't know about it. We'll be sure of avoiding interruption there."

"Felix—who *do* you work for?"

He held up the severed ear. "Suffice it to say—I'm against the owner of this."

I nodded. "I'll settle for that."

Three hours later, Felix switched off the light in the laboratory and led me into a comfortable lounge

room with teak paneling, deep chairs, a business-
like bar, and wide pseudowindows with a view of
a moonlit garden, which helped to dispel the oppressive feeling of being two hundred feet down. I
sat in one of the chairs and looked around me.

"Felix, who built this place? Somehow, this
doesn't look like a government-furnished installation to me. You've got equipment in that lab that's
ahead of anything I've seen. And you're not as
surprised at what I've told you as you ought to
be."

He leaned over and slapped me on the knee,
grinning his Mephistophelean grin. "Buck up,
Johnny. I sent you out to find an explanation of
something. You've found it—with bells on. If it
takes a few devil-dogs from Mars to tie it all together, that's not your fault."

"What the hell *did* I stumble into last night?"

He finished mixing drinks, sat down across from
me, rubbing the side of his jaw. The air-conditioners
made a faint hum in the background.

"It's the damnedest tissue I've ever examined.
Almost a crystalline structure. And the hairs! There
are metallic fibers in them; incredibly tough. The
fluid was a regular witches' brew; plenty of cyano-
globin present." He paused. "Something out of
this world, to coin a phrase."

"In other words, we've been invaded?"

"That's one way to put it—unless someone's invited them." He put his glass on the table at his
elbow, leaned forward.

"We know now that whatever it was that was
attached to the ear is responsible for the disappearance of men from battlefields—and other
places. From the number of such incidents, we can
surmise that there are hundreds—perhaps thousands—of these creatures among us."

"Why hasn't anybody seem them?"

"That's something we have to find out. Obviously, they employ some method of camouflage as they go about their work.

"Secondly, they've been busy among us for some time; missing-persons figures were unusually high as far back as World War One. The data for earlier conflicts are unreliable, but such as they are, they don't rule out the possibility."

"But why?"

"Apparently, these creatures have a use for human brain tissue. From the description you gave me, I surmise that the organ was in a nutrient solution of some sort—alive."

"My God."

"Yes. Now, we're faced with not one, but two varieties of adversary. It's plain that our former associate, General Julius, was something other than human."

"He looked as human as I do—maybe more so."

"Perhaps he is; modified, of course, to serve alien purposes. Some such arrangement would be necessary in order to carry on the day-to-day business . . ."

"What business—other than brain-stealing?"

"Consider for a moment: we know they've infiltrated the UN, and my hunch is we may find them in a lot of other places as well. From the speed with which they worked, it's obvious that they have a large, well-integrated operation—and methods of communication far more subtle than the clumsy apparatus we employ."

"There are five million people here, Felix; fifty governments are represented. I've only seen a couple of these supermen."

"True. But they say for every rat you see in the barnyard, there are a hundred more hiding somewhere." He looked almost pleased. "We're on our own, John. We can't shout for a policeman."

"What *can* we do? We're holed up under a hundred feet of shielded concrete, with plenty of food, liquor, and taped tri-D shows—but we might as well be locked in a cell."

Felix held up a hand. "We're not without resources, John. This hideaway was designed to provide the most complete and modern facilities for certain lines of research and testing. We know a few things about our aliens now—things they don't know we know. And I'm sure they're puzzling over your dramatic appearances and disappearances, much as we're pondering their capabilities. They're not super-beings. My little stinger killed one; you eluded others. Now that we know something of the nature of the enemy, we can begin to design counter-measures."

"Just two of us?"

"I didn't mean to imply that the enemy controls *everything*, John. It wouldn't be necessary; one or two cowboys can control quite a large herd of cattle . . ."

"Why herd us at all? Why not just round us up, chop out our brains, and let it go at that?"

"Oh, many reasons. Conservation of natural resources, ease of harvesting—and then, perhaps, we might not be quite safe, if we were once alerted to what was going on. Cattle have been known to stampede . . ."

"So—what do we do?"

"We leave Tamboula. Back in America, we make contact with a few individuals known to us personally. I'd steer clear of Barnett, for example, but there are a number of reliable men. Then we construct a counter-alien organization, armed and equipped—and then—well, we'll see."

"And how do we go about leaving Tamboula? I have an idea the whole scheme breaks down right there."

Felix looked sober. "I'm afraid our old friend Bravais will never be seen departing from these shores."

A small grin was tugging at the corners of his mouth. "I think he'll have to disappear in much the same manner that Major de Salle of the UN medical staff dropped from sight—and as one H. D. Brown, who leased the same house, will vanish one day soon."

"Behind a false beard and set of brown contact lenses?"

"Nothing so crude, my dear fellow." Felix was positively rubbing his hands together in anticipation. "I'm going to give you the full treatment— use some of those ideas they haven't been willing to give me guinea pigs for, up till now. You'll have a new hair color—self-regenerating, too—new eye color and retinal patterns, an inch or two difference in height, new finger- and dental-prints . . ."

"None of that will do me much good if some curious customs man digs under the dirty socks and finds that piece of ear. That's all the evidence we've got."

"Never fear, John. You won't be unprotected." There was a merry glint in his eye. "You won't merely have a new identity—I'm going to fit you out with full PAPA gear. If a General Julius jumps out at you then, just break him in two and keep going."

Chapter Six

I was sitting on the edge of a wooden chair, listening to a thin humming in my head.

"Tell me when the sound stops," Felix said. His voice seemed to be coming from a distance, even though I could see him standing a few feet away, looking hazy, like a photograph shot through cheesecloth. The buzzing grew fainter, faded . . .

I pressed the switch in my hand. Felix's blurred features nodded.

"Good enough, John. Now come around and let's check those ligament attachments."

I relaxed the muscles that had once been used to prick up the ears, thus switching my hearing range back to normal. I made a move to rise, and bounded three feet in the air.

"Easy, John." Felix had emerged from the cubicle with the two-inch-thick armorplast walls. "We can't have you springing about the room like a dervish. Remember your lessons."

I balanced carefully, like a man with springs

tied to his shoes. "I remember my lessons," I said. "Pain has a way of sticking in my mind."

"It's the best method when you're in a hurry."

"How did the test go?"

"Not badly at all. You held it to .07 microbel at 30,000 cycles. How was the vision?"

"About like shaving with a steamed mirror. I still get only blacks and whites."

"You'll develop a color discrimination after a while. Your optic center has been accustomed to just the usual six hues for thirty-odd years; it can't learn to differentiate in the ultraviolet range overnight."

"And I can't adjust to the feeling that I weigh half an ounce, either, dammit! I dance around on my toes like a barefooted hairdresser on a hot pavement."

Felix grinned as though I'd paid him a compliment. "In point of fact, you now weigh three hundred and twenty-eight pounds. I've plated another five mills of chromalloy onto the skeletal grid. Your system's shown a nice tolerance for it. I'm pulling one more net of the number nine web over the trapezius, deltoids, and latissimi dorsi—"

"The tolerances of my metabolism are not to be taken as those of the management," I cut in. "These past six weeks have been a vivisectionist's nightmare. I've got more scars than a Shendy tribesman, and my nerves are standing on end, waving around like charmed snakes. I'm ready to call it a day, and try it as is."

Felix nodded soberly. "We're about finished with you. I know it's been difficult, but there's no point in taking anything less than our best to the fray, is there?"

"I don't know why I don't ache all over," I grumbled. "I've been sliced, chiseled, and sawed at like a side of beef in a butcher's college. I suppose you've got me doped to the eyebrows; along with all the other strange sensations, a little thing like a neocaine jag would pass unnoticed."

"No—no dope; hypnotics, old boy."

"Swell. Every day in every way I'm hurting less and less, eh?"

I took a breath, more from habit than need; the oxygen storage units installed under the lower edge of my rib-cage were more than half charged; I could go for another two hours if I had to. "I know we're in a hell of a spot—and it's better to sail in with grins in place and all flags flying than sit around telling each other the crisis has arrived. But I'm ready for action."

Felix was looking at papers, paying no attention at all.

"Surely, old man. Gripe all you like," he said absently. "Just don't get friendly and slap me on the back. I'm still made of normal flesh and blood. Now, I'd like another check on the strain gauges."

"I closed my mouth and went across to the Iron Man—a collection of cables and bars that looked like an explosion in a bicycle factory.

"The grip, first."

I took the padded handle, settled my hand comfortably, squeezed lightly to get the feel of it, then put on the pressure. I heard a creak among the levers; then the metal collapsed like a cardboard in my hand.

I let go. "Sorry, Felix—but what the hell, thin-gauge aluminum—"

"That's a special steel tubing, cold-extruded, two tenths of an inch thick," Felix said, examining the wreckage. "Try a lift now."

I went over to a rig with a heavy horizontal beam. I bent my knees, settled my shoulders under it with a metal-to-wood clatter. I set myself, slowly straightened my legs. The pressure on my shoulders seemed modest—about like hefting a heavy suitcase. I came fully erect, then went up on my toes, pushing now against an almost immovable resistance.

"Slack off, John," Felix called. "I believe I'll consider you've passed your brute-strength test. Over twenty-nine hundred pounds—about what a Chevette runabout weighs—and I don't think you were flat out at that."

"I could have edged a few ounces more." I flexed my shoulders. "The padding helped, but it wasn't quite thick enough."

"The padding was two inches of oak." He looked at me, pulling at his lower lip. "Damned pity I can't take you along to the next Myoelectronics Congress; I could make a couple of blighters eat two-hour speeches saying it wasn't possible."

I took a turn up and down the room, trying not to bounce at each step.

"Felix, you said another week, to let the incisions heal. Let's skip that; I'm ready to go now. You've been in town every day and haven't seen any signs of abnormal activity. The alarm's died down."

"Died down too damned quickly to suit me," he snapped. "It's too quiet. At the least, I'd have expected someone out to check over the house. You'll recall that the former tenant, my alter ego, turned in a report on missing men and head wounds. But they haven't been near the place. There's been nothing in the papers since the first day or two— and I daresay it wouldn't have been mentioned then, except that a crowd of idlers saw you kill Julius."

"Look, Felix; I've got so damned much microtronics gear buried in my teeth I'm afraid to eat anything tougher than spaghetti; I've got enough servo-motors bolted to my insides to power an automatic kitchen. Let's skip the rest of the program and get going. I may have new stainless-steel knuckles, but it's the same old me inside. I'm getting the willies. I want to know what those hell-hounds are doing up there."

"What time is it?" Felix asked suddenly.

I glanced at the black-and-white wall clock. "Twenty-four minutes after nine," I said.

Felix raised his hand and snapped his fingers—

I felt a slight twitch—as though everything in the room had jumped half an inch. Felix was looking at me with a quizzical smile.

"What time did you say it was?"

"Nine twenty-four."

"Look at the clock."

I glanced at it again. "Why, is it—" I stopped. The hands stood at ten o'clock.

"Clock manipulation at a distance," I said. "How do you do it—and why?"

Felix shook his head, smiling. "You've just had another half-hour session in deep hypnosis, John. I want another couple of days to reinforce that primary personality fraction I've split off, before I tie it in with a mnemonic cross-connection. We want your alter ego to be sure to swing into action at the first hint of outside mental influences."

"Speaking of psychodynamics, how are you coming along with your own conditioning?"

"Pretty well, I think. I've been attempting to split off a personality fraction for myself. I'm not sure how effective my efforts have been. Frankly, autohypnosis was never my strong suit. Still, there are a few facts that I can't afford to expunge from my mind completely—but on the other hand, I can't afford to let the enemy have them. I've buried them in the alternate ego, and keyed them to a trigger word. The same word is tied to my heart action.

"In other words—if anyone cues this information, it's suicide for you."

"Correct," Felix said cheerfully. "I need the basic power of the survival instinct to cover this information. I've given you the key word under hypnosis. Your subconscious will know when to use it."

"Pretty drastic, isn't it?"

"It's tricky business, trying to outguess a virtually unknown enemy; but from their interest in brains, it's a fair guess that they know a bit about the mechanics of the human mind. We can't rule out the possibility that they possess a technique for controlling human mental processes. I can't let them control mine. I've got too many secrets."

I chewed that one over. "You may be right. That tank driver didn't behave like a man who was running his own affairs. And whatever it was that hit him—and the major—"

"It could have been an amplified telepathic command—to stop breathing, perhaps—or shutting off the flow of blood through the carotid arteries. From the fact that it didn't affect you, we can assume that their technique is selective; it probably requires at least a visual fix on the object, for a start."

"We're assuming a hell of a lot, Felix. We'd better do some more fieldwork before we reason ourselves right out onto the end of a long limb."

Felix was looking thoughtful. "It shouldn't be too difficult to arrange shielding around the personality center area; a platinum-gauge micro-grid with a filament spacing of about—"

"Oh-oh. This sounds like another expedition into the seat of what I once thought of as my intelligence."

Felix clucked. "I can handle it with a number 27 probe, like building a ship in a bottle. It could make a great difference—if it works."

"There's too much guesswork here, Felix."

"I know." He nodded. "But we've got to extract every possible ounce of intelligence on the enemy from the few fragments of data we have. I don't think we're going to have much in the way of a second chance."

"We'll be doing well if we have a first one."

"You *are* getting nervous."

"You're damned right! If I don't get going soon, I may funk the whole act and retire to a small farm near Nairobi to write my memoirs."

Felix cackled. "Let's dial ourselves a nice little *entrecôte avec champignons* and a liter or two of a good burgundy, and forget business for an hour or two. Give me three more days, John; then we'll make our play—ready or not."

The night air was cold and clean; gravel crunched under my feet with a crisp, live sound. Felix tossed our two small bags in the boot of the car, paused to sniff the breeze.

"A fine night for trouble," he said briskly.

I looked up at the spread of fat, multicolored stars. "It's good to be out, after fifty days of stale air and scalpels," I said. "Trouble or no trouble." I slid into my seat, taking care not to bend any metal.

"We'll have to register you as a lethal weapon when this caper is over," Felix said, watching me gingerly fasten my seat belt. "Meantime, watch what you grab if I take a corner a trifle too fast." He started up, pulled off down the drive, turned into the highway.

"It's not too late to change plans and take the Subsea Tube to Naples," I said. "I have a negative vibration when it comes to rocket flights; why not go underground, the way the Lord intended us to travel?"

"I won the deck-cut, old boy," Felix said. "For myself, I've had enough of the underground life; I want a fast transit to New York."

"I feel a little exposed right now," I said. "Too bad we don't have two OE suits."

"Wouldn't help if we did; you couldn't wear one aboard an aircraft, tube, or anything else without showing up on a dozen different monkey-business detectors. But we'll be all right. They aren't looking for me—and your own mistress wouldn't know you now. You're good-looking, boy!"

"I know; I'm just talking to keep myself occupied."

"You have our prize exhibit all cozy in your trick belt?"

"Yep."

We drove in silence for the next mile. The city lights glowed on our right as we swung off on the port road. We pulled into a mile-wide lot under banked poly-arcs, then rode a slipway to the rotunda—a glass-walled arena under a paper-thin airfoil, cantilevered out in hundred-yard wings from supporting columns of ferro-concrete twelve feet thick at the base. I concentrated on walking without hopping, while Felix led the way across to an island of brighter lights and polished counters, where showgirls in trim uniforms stamped tickets and gave discouraging answers to male passengers with three-hour layovers to kill.

I watched the crowd while he went through the formalities. There were the usual fat ladies in paint and finger rings; slim, haughty women with strange-looking hats; bald businessmen with wilting linen and a mild glow expensively acquired at the airport bar; damp-looking recruits in rumpled uniforms; thin official travelers with dark suits, narrow shoulders, and faces as expressive as filing cabinets.

Once I spotted a big black and tan German shepherd on a leash, and I twitched; my foot hit a parked suitcase, sent it cannonballing against the counter. Felix stepped in quickly, soothed the fat man who owned the mishandled luggage, and guided me toward a glass stairway that swept up to a gallery lined with live-looking palms. We headed for a pair of frosted glass doors under three-foot glare-letters reading *Aloha Room* in flowing script.

"We have nearly an hour before takeoff; time for a light snack and a stirrup cup." Felix seemed to be in the best of spirits now; the fresh air had revived me, too. The sight of the normally milling crowds, the air of business-like bustle, the bright lights made the memories of stealthy horrors seem remote.

We took a table near the far side of the wide, mosaic-floored, softly-lit room. A smiling waitress in leis and a grass skirt took orders for martinis. Across the room, a group of dark, bowlegged men with flamboyant shirts and large smiles strummed guitars.

Felix glanced around contentedly. "I think perhaps we've overestimated the opposition, John." He lit up a dope-stick, blew violet smoke toward an ice-bucket by the next table. "Another advantage of rocket travel is the champagne," he remarked. "We can be nicely oiled by the time we fire retros over Kennedy—"

"While we're overestimating the enemy, let's not forget that he has a number of clever tricks we haven't quite mastered yet," I put in. "Getting out of Tamboula is a start, but we still have the problem of contact when we reach the States. We won't accomplish much hiding out in back rooms over tamale joints, sneaking out at night for a pictonews to find out what's going on."

Felix nodded. "I have some ideas on that score. We'll also need a quick and inconspicuous method of identifying 'human' aliens. I think I know how that can be done. We can work with the radar albedo of the alien skin, for example; it must be a rather unusual material to withstand puncturing steel doors."

He was smiling again, looking happy. He leaned

toward me, talking against a strident voice from the next table.

"I've been working for twenty years, preparing for what I've termed a 'surreptitious war,' based on the premise that when the next conflict took place, it would be fought not on battlefields, or in space, but in the streets and offices of apparently peaceful cities—a war of brainwashing techniques, infiltration, subversion, betrayal. It's been in the air for a hundred years: a vast insanity that's kept us flogging away, nation against nation, race against race—with the planets at our fingertips . . ."

Something was happening. The music was changing to a sour whine in my ears. The chatter at the tables around me was like the petulant cries of trapped monkeys in vast, bleak cages.

Felix was still talking, jabbing with a silver spoon to emphasize his points. My eyes went to the double doors fifty yards distant across the brittle-patterned floor. Beyond the dark glass, shapes moved restlessly, like dim shadows of crawling men . . .

I pushed my chair back. "Felix!" I croaked.

". . . could have established a permanent colony of perhaps five thousand. Carefully picked personnel, of course—"

"The door!" My voice was choking off in my throat. The air in the room seemed to darken; tiny points of light danced before me.

"Something wrong, old boy?" Felix was leaning forward, a concerned expression on his face. He looked as unreal now as a paper cutout—a cardboard man in a cardboard scene.

Far across the room, the doors swung silently open. A staring corpse-pale face appeared, at the level of a man's belt. It pushed into the room, the long, lean bristled body pacing on legs like the arms of apes, the fingered feet slapping the floor in a deliberate rhythm. A second beast followed, smaller, with a blacker coat and a grayish ruff edging the long-toothed face. A third and fourth passed through the door, both rangy, heavy, their long bodies sagging between humped shoulders and lean flanks. The leader raised his head, seeming to sniff the air.

"Felix!" I pointed.

He turned casually, let his gaze linger a moment, then glanced at me with a slight smile.

"Very attractive," he said. "You must be recovering, John, for a pretty face to excite you—"

"Good God, Felix! Can't you see them?"

He frowned. "You're shouting, John. Yes, I saw them." I was aware of faces turning toward me at the surrounding tables, eyebrows raised, frowns settling into place. I reached out, caught Felix's arm; his face contorted in a spasm of agony.

"Felix—you've got to listen. What do you see coming through that door?"

"Four young women," he said in a choked voice, "very gay, very sweet. Would that I had time . . ." His face was paling. "John, you're breaking my arm—"

I jerked my hand back. "They're aliens, Felix! The dog things I saw in the ravine! Look again! Try to see them!"

The leading demon had turned toward us now; the white face was fixed on me as it came on, steadily, relentlessly, stalking unnoticed along the aisle between the tables where diners laughed and talked, forking food into overfed mouths.

Felix turned, stared. "They're coming toward us," he said in a voice thin with strain. "The first young lady is dressed in yellow—"

"It's a thing like a tailless dog; a skull-face, stiff black hair. Remember the ear?"

Felix tensed; an uncertain expression crept over his face. He turned toward me.

"I—" he started. His features went slack; his

head lolled, eyes half-open. The music died with a squawk. Conversation drained into silence.

The first of the monstrosities quickened its pace; its head came up as it headed straight for me. I leaned toward Felix, shouted his name. He muttered something, slumped back, stared vacantly past me.

"Felix, for God's sake, use your gun!" I jumped up, and my knee caught the table; it went flying against the next one. Felix tumbled back, slammed to the floor. I caught a momentary impression of dull-faced patrons, sitting slackly at tables all around. There was a quickening slap of beast-hands now as the leading thing broke into a clumsy gallop, closing now, red eyes glinting, the black tongue lolling from the side of the wide jaws as it cleared the last few yards, sprang—

With a shout of horror, I swung my right fist in a round-house blow that caught the monster squarely in the neck, sent it crashing across a table in an explosion of silver, glasses, and laden plates to go down between tables in a tangle of snowy linen. Then the second demonic thing was on me. I saw dagger-teeth flash, ducked aside, caught a thick forearm, feeling the flesh tear under my hand as I hurled it aside. The beast whirled, squealing thinly, reared up seven feet tall—

I struck at it, saw its face collapse into pulped ruin. It fell past me, kicking frantically. The last two attackers split, rushed me from both sides. I ran toward the one on the left, missed a swing at its head, felt the impact of its weight like a feather mattress, the clamp of teeth on my arm. I staggered, caught myself, slammed blows at the bristled side; it was like pounding a saddle. I struck for the head then, saw skin and flesh shear under the impact, struck again, knocked an eye from its socket—

And still the thing clung, raking at me with its

pale hands like minstrel's gloves. I reached for its throat with my free hand, whirled to interpose its body between me and the last of the four creatures as it sprang; the impact knocked me back a step, sent the attacker sprawling. It leaped up, slunk around to the left of a fallen table to take me from the side.

At that moment, to my horror, the music resumed. I heard a tinkle of laughter, an impatient call for a waiter. Beyond the crushed head at my arm, with its single hate-filled eye, I caught a glimpse of the animated faces of diners, busy forks, a raised wine-glass—

"Help me, for the love of God!" I roared. No one so much as glanced in my direction. I ripped at the locked jaws on my arm, feeling bone and leather shred and crumble. With a sound like nails tearing from wood, the fangs scraped clear, shredding my sleeve; the long body fell back, slack. I threw it aside, turned to face the last of the monsters. Baleful red eyes in a white mask of horror stared at me across a table ten feet away where a man with a red-veined nose sniffed a glass thoughtfully. On the floor at my feet, Felix lay half under the body of a dead demon.

Now the last of the four creatures moved in. Beyond it, I saw a movement at the entrance; the door swung wide. Two demons came through it at a run, then another—

The thing nearest me crouched back, wide mouth gaping. It had learned a measure of caution now; I took a step back, looked around for a route of escape—

"*Now!*" a silent voice seemed to shout in my mind. "*Now . . . !*"

I took my eyes from the death's head that snarled three yards away, fixed my eyes on Felix's face.

"Ashurbanipal!" I shouted.

Felix's eyes opened—dead eyes in a corpse's face.

"The Franklin Street Postal Station in Coffeyville, Kansas," he said in a lifeless monotone. "Box 1742, Code—"

There was a rasp of horny fingers on the floor, a blur of movement as the demon sprang; it landed full on Felix's chest, and I saw its boned snout go down . . .

I threw myself at it, grappled the bristled torso to me, felt bones collapse as we smashed against a table, sent it crashing. I kicked the dead thing aside, scrambled up to see a pack of its fellows leaping to the attack, more boiling through the open doors. I caught a glimpse of Felix, blood covering his chest—then I leaped clear and ran.

Far across the wide room, tall glass slabs reared up thirty feet to the arched ceiling. Tables bounded to left and right as I cut a swath across the crowded floor. Ten feet from the wall, I crossed my arms over my face, lowered my head, and dived.

There was a shattering crash as the glass exploded from its frame; I felt a passing sting as huge shards tumbled aside. There was a moment of whipping wind; then I slammed against the concrete terrace as lightly as a straw man. I rolled, came to my feet, sprinted for the darkness beyond the lighted plaza.

Behind me, glass smashed; I heard the thud of heavy bodies spilling through the opening, the scrabble of feet. People whirled from my path with little screams; then I was past them, dashing across a spread of lawn, then crashing through underbrush like spiderwebs and into the clear. In the bright moonlight the stony desert stretched to the seacliffs a mile distant.

Behind me, I heard the relentless gallop of demonic pursuers. In my mind was the image of the comrade I had left behind—the incomparable Felix, dead beneath a tidal wave of horrors.

I ran—and the Hounds of Hell bayed behind me.

Chapter Seven

I huddled in a sea-carved hollow at the base of a crumbling twenty-foot cliff of sandy clay, breathing in vast gulps of cold, damp air, hearing the slap and hiss of the surf that curled in phosphorescent sheets almost to my feet. Far out on the black Mediterranean, gleaming points of light winked on the horizon—ships lying to anchor in the roadstead off Tamboula.

I pulled my coat off, peeled my blood-stiffened shirt from my back. By the light of the moon I examined the gouges across my left forearm, made by the demon's teeth. Tiny gleaming filaments of metal showed in the cuts; the thing's fangs had been as hard as diamond.

Cold night wind whipped at me. Felix hadn't thought to install any insulation in the course of the remodeling. I tore a sleeve from my shirt, bound up my arm. There were cuts on my face and shoulders from the glass; not deep, and thanks to Felix's hypnotic commands, not painful—but blood was

71

flowing freely. I got to my feet and waded out ankle-deep, scooped cold salt water on my wounds, then pulled my shirt and coat back on. It was all I could do in the way of first aid. Now it was time to give my attention to survival.

I didn't know how many miles I had run—or how far behind the dog-things trailed me. I keened my hearing, breath stopped, hoping there would be nothing but the sigh of the wind . . .

Far across the plain, I heard the slap of galloping beast-hands—how many, I couldn't tell. There was a chance that if I stayed where I was, in the shelter of the cliff, they might pass me by—but they had come unerringly to me as I sat in the bright-lit restaurant with Felix . . .

I wouldn't wait here, to be cornered in the dark; better to meet them in the open, kill as many as I could before they pulled me down.

There was a narrow strip of wet, boulder-dotted beach running along the base of the sheer wall behind me. I went a few yards along it, splashing through shallow pools; an earth-fall had made a shelving slope to the level ground above.

At the top, I lay flat, looked out across the plain. I saw that I was at the tip of a tongue of desert thrusting out into the sea, a narrow peninsula no more than a hundred yards wide at its base. Far away, the city was a pink glow against the sky; near at hand, I saw dark shapes that could have been rocks—or crouching enemies.

I squinted down hard to trigger my visual booster complex. The desert sprang into instant, vivid clarity. Every stone fragment, mesquite bush, darting ground rat, stood out as under a full moon . . .

A hundred yards away, a long, dark-glistening creature bounded from the shelter of a rock slab, swinging its pale, snouted face from right to left as it ran. Over the roar of the surf, the distant whir and clatter of night-locusts, the pad of its feet was loud; its breathing was a vile intimacy in my ears.

When the thing was fifty feet away, it stopped abruptly, one white hand raised. Its gleaming eyes turned toward my hiding place. It leaped straight toward me.

I came to my feet, caught up a head-sized rock that seemed as light as cork, threw it. It slammed off the creature's flank with a sound like a brick hitting a board fence, knocked it off its feet—but the thing was up in an instant, leaping across the last few yards . . .

I leaned aside, swung a kick that went home with a thud, then chopped a bone-smashing blow behind the shoulder ruff, felt the spine shatter. The thing struck heavily, rolled, lay for a moment, stunned. Then the head came up; it moved feebly, scrabbling with its front legs. I felt the skin prickle along the back of my neck.

"What are you?" I called hoarsely. "Where do you come from? What do you want?"

The ruby eyes held on my face; the broken body lunged forward another foot.

"You understand me—can't you speak?"

Still it dragged itself on, its jaws smiling their skull-smile. The smell of its blood was a poison-chemical reek. I looked back toward the city. Far away, I saw movement—low shapes that galloped silently. From all across the barren plain they streamed toward the point of land where I stood, summoned by the dying creature at my feet.

I stood at the edge of the cliff above the breaking surf, watching them come. It was useless to run any farther. Even if I escaped the trap I had entered, there was no refuge along the coast; Algiers was sixty miles to the east. To the west, there was nothing between me and Oran, over a hundred miles away. I could run for half an hour, cover perhaps twenty miles, before oxygen starvation would force me to stop; but the aliens would follow with the patience of death.

Out across the dark water, the nearest ship lay no more than two miles offshore. The dog-things were close now. I could see them silhouetted against the lesser sky-glow, like some evil swarm of giant rats piped from their lair by the music of hell—a plague of demons. The leaders slowed, coming on cautiously, dozens of them, almost shoulder to shoulder . . .

I turned, leaped far out toward the black surf below. I felt the icy waters close over me. Swimming just above the muddy bottom, I struck out for deep water, heading out to sea.

The ocean floor by night was a magic land of broken terrain, darting schools of many-colored fishes, waving screens of green, translucent weed. A hundred feet from shore, the bottom fell away, and I swept out over a dark chasm, feeling the chill currents of deep water as I angled downward. The small fish disappeared. A great, dark, lazy shape sailed toward me out of the blackness, was swallowed up in the gloom. There were noises; grunts, shrill whistles, the grind and thud of tide-stirred rocks on the bottom, the distant, mechanical whirring of a propeller-driven boat.

After twenty minutes, my vision began to blur; I was feeling the strain in my arms, and the first stifling sensations of oxygen starvation. I angled upward, broke the surface, and saw the low silhouette of a half-submerged vessel a quarter of a mile away across rippled ink-and-silver water, streaked with the winking reflections of her deck lights.

I trod water, looking around; a bell-buoy clanged a hundred yards away. Farther off, a small boat buzzed toward shore from a ship in the distance. There was a smell of sea-things, salt, a metallic

odor of ship's engines, a vagrant reek of oil. There
was no sign of pursuit from the shore.

I swam on toward the ship, came up on her from
the starboard quarter, and made out the words
EXCALIBUR—New Hartford in raised letters across
her stern. There was a deck-house beyond a low
guard rail, a retractable antenna array perched
atop it with crimson and white lights sparkling at
the peak.

Farther forward, small deck cranes poised over
an open hatch like ungainly herons waiting for a
minnow. I caught a faint sound of raucous music,
a momentarily raised voice. The odor of petroleum
was strong here, and there was a glistening scum
on the water. She was a tanker, loaded and ready
to sail, to judge from the waterline, a foot above
her anachronistic plimsoll.

I pulled myself up on the corroding hull-plates,
inched my way to the rail, crossed to the deck-
house. The door opened into warmth, light, the
odors of beer, tobacco smoke, unlaundered humans.
I took a great, grateful lungful; this was familiar,
reassuring—the odor of my kind of animal.

Steep stairs led down. I followed them, came
into a narrow corridor with a three-inch glare-
strip along the center line of the low ceiling. There
were doors set at ten-foot intervals along the
smooth, buff-colored walls. Voices muttered at the
far end of the corridor. I stepped to the nearest
door, listened with my hearing keened, then turned
the handle and stepped inside.

It was an eight-by-ten cell papered with photo-
murals of Central Park, chipped and grease-stained
at hand level. There was a table, a metal locker, a
hooked rug on the floor, a tidy bunk, a single-tube
lamp clamped to the wall above it beside a hand-
painted plaster plaque representing a haloed saint
with a dazed expression.

Footsteps were coming along the corridor. I turned to the door as it opened, and nearly collided with a vast, tall man in a soiled undershirt bulging with biceps, blue trousers worn low to ease a paunch that looked slight against his massive bulk.

He stared down at me, frowning; he had curly, uncut hair, large, dull-brown eyes, a loose mouth. There was a deeply depressed scar the size of an egg on the side of his forehead above his left eye. He raised a hand, pointed a thick finger at me.

"Hey!" he said, in a startlingly mellow tenor. He blinked past me at the room. "This here is *my* flop."

"Sorry," I said. "I guess I kind of stumbled into the wrong place." I started past him. He moved slightly, blocking the door.

"How come you're in my flop?" he demanded. He didn't sound mad—just mildly curious.

"I was looking for the Mate," I said. "He must be down the hall, eh?"

"Heck, no; the Mate got a fancy place aft." He was looking me over now. "How come you're all wet?"

"I fell in the water," I said. "Look, how are you fixed for crew aboard this ship?"

The giant reached up, rasped at his scalp with a fingernail like a banjo pick.

"You want to sign on?"

"Right. Now—"

"Who you want to see, you want to see Carboni. Oh, boy . . ." the loose mouth curved in a vast grin. "He'll be surprised, all right. Nobody don't want to sign on aboard the *'Scabbler.'*"

"Well, *I* do. Where do I find him?"

The grin dropped. "Huh?"

"Where can I find Mr. Carboni—so I can sign on, you know?"

The grin was back. He nodded vigorously. "He's prob'ly down in the ward room. He's prob'ly pretty drunk."

"Maybe you could show me the way."

He looked blank for a moment, then nodded. "Yeah. Hey." He was frowning again, looking at my shoulder. "You got a cut on ya. You got a couple cuts. You been in a fight?"

"Nothing serious. How about Mr. Carboni?"

The finger was aimed at me like a revolver. "That's how come you want to sign on the 'Scabbler. I betcha you croaked some guy, and the cops is after ya."

"Not as far as I know, big boy. Now—"

"My name ain't Big Boy; it's Joel."

"Okay, Joel. Let's go see the man, all right?"

"Come on." He moved out of the doorway, started off along the corridor, watching to be sure I was following.

"Carboni, he drinks a couple of bottles and he gets drunk. I tried that, but it don't work. One time I drank two bottles of booze but all it done, it made me like burp."

"When does the ship sail?"

"Huh? I dunno."

"What's your destination?"

"What's that?"

"Where's the ship going?"

"Huh?"

"Skip it, Joel. Just take me to your leader."

After a five-minute walk along crisscrossing passageways, we ducked our heads, stepped into a long, narrow room where three men sat at an oilcloth-covered table decorated with a capless ketchup bottle and a mustard pot with a wooden stick. There were four empty liquor bottles on the table, and another, nearly full one.

The drinker on the opposite side of the table looked up as we came in. He was a thick-necked fellow with a bald head, heavy features, bushy eyebrows, a blotchy complexion. He sat slumped with both arms on the table encircling his glass. One of his eyes looked at the ceiling with a mild expression; the other fixed itself on me. A frown made a crease between the eyes.

"Who the hell are you?" His voice was a husky whisper; someone had hit him in the windpipe once, but it hadn't improved his manners.

I stepped up past Joel. "I want to sign on for the cruise."

He swallowed a healthy slug of what was in the glass, glanced at his companions, who were hitching around to get a look at me.

"He says it's a cruise," he rasped. "He wants to sign on, he says." The eye went to Joel. "Where'd you pick this bird up?"

Joel said, "Huh?"

"Where'd you come from, punk?" The eye was back on me again. "How'd you get aboard?"

"The name's Jones," I said. "I swam. What about that job?"

"A job, he says." The eye ran over me. "You're a seaman, eh?"

"I can learn."

"He can learn, he says."

"Not many guys want to sign on this tub, do they, Carboni?" Joel asked brightly.

"Shut up," Carboni growled without looking at him. "You got blood on your face," he said to me.

I put a hand up, felt a gash across my jaw.

"I don't like this mug's looks," one of the drinking buddies said, in a voice like fingernails on a blackboard. He was a long-faced, lanky, big-handed fellow in grimy whites. He had a large nose, coarse skin, long, discolored teeth with receding gums.

"A chain-climber. I got a good mind to throw

him to hell off back in the drink where he come from. He looks like some kind of cop to me."

"Do I get the job or not?" I said, looking at Carboni.

"I'm talking to you, mug," the long man said. "I ast you if you're a cop."

"Who runs this show?" I said, still watching Carboni. "You or this talking horse?" I jerked a thumb at the second man. He made an explosive noise, started up from the bench.

"Sit down, Pogey," Carboni snarled. The lanky man sank back, talking to himself.

"That's a pretty good swim out from shore," Carboni said. "You musta been in a pretty big hurry to leave town."

I didn't say anything.

"Cops after you?"

"Not that I know of."

"Not that he knows of, he says." Carboni grinned. He had even white teeth; they looked as though they had cost a lot of money.

"Any papers?"

I shook my head.

"No papers, he says."

"You want me I should pitch 'im over the side, Carboni?" the third man asked. He was a swarthy man with stubby arms and a crooked jaw, like a dwarfed giant.

"Cap'n wouldn't like that," Joel said. "Cap'n said we needed crew—"

"Up the Captain's," the horsey man said. "We don't need no—"

"Pogey." Carboni rolled the eye over to bear on him. "You talk too much. Shut up." He jolted his chair back, turned, lifted a phone off a wall bracket, thumbed a call button. The glass eye was rolled over my way now, as though watching for a false move.

"Skipper, I got a bird here says he's a seaman," Carboni said into the instrument. "Claims he lost his papers ..." There was a pause. "Yeah," Carboni said. "Yeah ..." He listened again, then hitched himself up in the chair, frowning. He glanced toward me.

"Yeah?" he said.

I let my gaze wander idly across the room, and switched my hearing into high gear. Background noises leaped into crackling presence; the hum of the phone was a sharp whine. I heard wood and metal creak, the thump of beating hearts, the glutinous wheeze of lungs expanding, the heavy grate of feet shifting on the floor—and faintly, an excited voice:

"... *UN radio* ... *a guy* ... *bumped off somebody* ... *Maybe a couple* ... *try for a ship, they said. Cripes, looks like* ..."

Felix had said that with a little concentration, I could develop selectivity. I needed it now. I strained to filter the static, catch the words:

"... *handle him?*"

Carboni looked my way again. "Can a kid handle a lollipop?"

"Okay ... look ..." The voice was clearer now. "... *lousy local cops* ... *we turn this guy in* ... *reward, peanuts* ... *their problem. We need hands. Okay, we work this boy* ... *get there* ... *Stateside cops* ... *a nice piece of change* ..."

"I see what you mean, Skipper," Carboni said. He had a corner of his mouth lifted to show me a smile that I might have found reassuring if I'd been a female crocodile.

"*Get him down below* ... *Anchors in in an hour and a half. Shake it up.*"

"Leave it to me, Skipper." Carboni hung up, swung around to give me the full-face smile. The bridgework wasn't so expensive after all—just old-style removable plates.

"Well, I decided to give you a chance, Jones," he croaked. "You're on. You'll sign papers in the morning."

"Hey, okay if he helps me out in the hot-room and stuff?" Joel asked. He sounded like a ten-year-old asking for a puppy.

Carboni thrust out his lips, nodded. "All right, Jones; for now, you help the dummy. Take the flop next to his."

"By the way, where's this tub headed?" I asked.

"Jacksonville. Why? You choosy or something?"

"If I was, would I be here?"

Carboni snorted. "Anchors in in an hour." He leveled the eye on Joel. "Get moving," he barked. "What do you think this is, a rest home for morons?"

"Come on." Joel tugged at my arm. I followed him out, along corridors to a door. He opened it, flipped on a light, showed me a room identical with his own except that it lacked the plaster saint and the hooked rug. He opened the locker, tossed sheets and a blanket on the bed. I pulled off my wet jacket. Joel puckered his mouth, looking at me.

"Hey, Jones, you better get Doc to fix them cuts you got."

I sat on the bunk. I felt weak suddenly, sucked as dry as a spider's dinner. There was a humming in the back of my head, and my face felt hot. I pulled the sodden, makeshift bandage from the arm the dog-thing had chewed. There were four deep gouges, half a dozen shallower ones—all inflamed, swelling. The arm was hot and painful.

"Can you get me some antiseptic and tape?" I asked.

"Huh?"

"Is there a first-aid kit around?"

Joel pondered, then went into the corridor, came back with a blue-painted metal box.

In it, I found a purple fluid that bubbled when I daubed my wounds. Joel watched, fascinated. At my request, he applied some to the cuts on my back, working with total concentration, his mouth hanging open. If he saw the glint of metal filaments in the torn skin, he made no comment.

I folded gauze; Joel helped me tape it in place. When we finished, he stood back, smiling. Then he frowned.

"Hey, Jones—how come you didn't get Doc to fix you up?"

"I'll be okay," I said.

Joel nodded, as though I had clarified a difficult point. He looked at me, frowning. He was thinking again.

"How come Carboni's scared of you?" he asked.

"He's not scared of me, Joel," I said. "He took a shine to me on sight."

Joel thought that one over. "Yeah," he said. "But look; we got stuff we got to do. We got to get a move on."

I stood up, acutely aware of fatigue, and wounds, and a sensation similar to a ticking bomb behind my eyes. Felix's posthypnotic anesthetic had been a big help while it lasted, but the withdrawal symptoms evened the score.

"I want to go up on deck a minute," I said. Joel blinked, followed me. I stepped out onto the deck, shivered in my wet clothes as the freshening wind hit me. There were no lights on the shore opposite; half a mile to the left, there was a faint gleam from the windows of beach shacks. Farther along, the great arc of the dredged harbor was a line of jewels against the night.

I tensed the eye-squint muscles, saw the black water snap into gray, misty clarity. On its surface, nothing stirred. I attuned my hearing to pick up the softest of night sounds. There were the thousand pings and thumps from the ship, the creak of the anchor cables, and the *crump!* and hiss of the distant surf. If the demons were close, they were well hidden. For the moment, it seemed, I was safe.

Chapter Eight

For the first eight hours at my new job, while the ancient tanker plowed at fifty knots sixty-five feet beneath the surface of the Mediterranean, I labored with Joel at routine drudgery that could have been performed with greater efficiency and less cost by a medium-priced computer.

I spent a bad hour when we surfaced to pass through the Gibraltar locks; a boat came alongside and I heard the clank of feet on the deck above, caught scraps of voices asking questions, and the Captain blandly denying any knowledge of stowaways. I was waiting just inside the deckhouse door as he invited his official visitors to search the ship. They declined, with curses. I heard them reboard their launch; then the sound of its engines growled away across the water. I leaned against the wall, feeling hot and dizzy. My arm throbbed like a giant toothache.

Joel had been waiting with me. "Hey, Jones," he

said. "How come we're hanging around here? You going out on deck?"

I let a long breath out; it was a bad habit I was forming—forgetting to breathe for minutes at a stretch. I straightened with an effort, feeling the deck move under me. "Sure," I said. "Let's go take a look at the Rock."

The cold predawn air cleared my head. I leaned on the rail beside Joel, watching the towering barrier walls slip down into the churning water as the lock filled; then the tanker edged ahead, the mighty gates slid in behind us, churning water aside, and met with a dull boom.

Again we rode the flood, gained another hundred feet. Forty-five minutes and five locks later, we slid out into the choppy, blue-black waters of the South Atlantic, five hundred feet above the level of the Mediterranean. Dawn was coloring the sky. Lights gleamed wanly from the fortress of Gibraltar, and from the flat, white city on the African side.

A raucous buzzer sounded across the deck. At once, the foaming water surged higher along the hull.

"Hey, we better get below before we get dunked," Joel said. We stepped back into the stale interior; a moment later we heard the crash of the waters closing over us above; then the silence of the deep sea settled in again.

"Well," Joel said cheerfully. "I guess we got to get back to work, Jones."

During the next forty-eight hours, Joel and I found time for several four-hour sleeps and a couple of short naps, between bellowed orders from Carboni or the unseen Captain. At odd intervals, we went to the crew mess, demanded and got plates of oily cold-storage eggs and too-salty bacon.

Now, having just completed a laborious two-hour visual inspection of reset switches, I again sat at the long table, listening to the feverish humming in my head, picking at a mixture of mummified beef and canned milk and taking medicinal sips from a clay mug of North African brandy. Across the table, the bearded elder known as Doc worked conscientiously to finish the bottle.

Joel had put his head on the table and gone off to sleep. At the far end of the room, Pogey, the horsefaced man, was monotonously and with much profanity calling off items from an inventory list, while a short, chinless sailor with a wool cap and warts ticked them off on a clipboard.

What the rest of the nine-man crew did aboard the vessel, I hadn't yet learned. Four of them had just left the room, staggering drunk.

"Three more trips, Jones," Doc said. "Thirty-one years on the line—nine on *Excalibur*; I'll miss the old tub." He looked around the room with sad, red-veined eyes. "No, I'm a liar," he corrected. "I hate this damned scow." He looked at me as though I had praised it. "I've hated every minute of those thirty-one years. Hated medical school before that. You ever been in a cadaver lab?"

"Sure have," I said, forcing myself to follow the conversation. "There was a fellow I hadn't seen for years. Opened up the tin box, and there he was." I sipped the brandy, feeling it burn its way down. Doc worked his lips, blinked, took a pull at his drink.

"I knew a fellow," he said, "sold his body to a medical school. Got five hundred cees for it, which he badly needed at the time. Later on, he got in the chips, and thought better of the bargain. Wanted to buy it back. Well, seems like the title had changed hands a couple of times. He traced it from New Haven to Georgia, and on down to Miami. Finally caught up with it." He took a healthy draught from his cup, exhaled noisily. "Too late, though. End of the year, you know. Nothing left but a few ribs, the left arm, and the bottom half of the cranium." He sighed. "A sad case."

His image was wavering, obscured by whirling points of light; I blinked them away, raised my glass to him. "Doc, you're one of the finest liars I ever met."

He blushed, looking modest. "Shucks, seems like things just naturally happen to me. Why, I remember the time . . ." At the far end of the table, Pogey tossed his list aside, yawned, scratched at an unshaven jaw.

"Get some coffee over here, Runt," he ordered. The warty sailor bustled, operating the coffee maker. He filled a two-quart pot, rattled thick cups and sheet-metal spoons. He placed the pot in front of the horse-faced man.

"Watch out, Mr. Dobbin. She's plenty hot." He went back to his list, muttering to himself.

Pogey grunted. He glanced at Joel, snoring across the table from him. He licked a finger, touched it to the polished metal; it hissed. An expression twitched at the corners of his mouth. He took the pot gingerly by the massive insulated handle, stood.

"Hey, dummy!" he said sharply.

Joel stirred.

"Wake up, dummy!"

Joel sat up, knuckling his eyes. He saw Pogey and smiled.

"Gee, I guess I—"

"Here!" Pogey thrust the pot at him. Joel reached out, took the rounded container in his two huge hands. His jaw dropped. His eyes widened. Pogey stepped back, his mouth arched in a grin like something carved at the top of Notre Dame.

I was a little slow, but I reached Joel then, knocked the steaming pot from his hands; it smashed against the wall behind Pogey, spewed steam and liquid in a wide sheet that caught the horse-faced man all across the back.

He howled, writhed away from the table, clutching at his shoulder. He screamed again, tore at his jacket. Doc came to his feet, grabbing at the bottle as it tottered, almost fell. The horse-faced man clawed his shirt open, ripped it from his shoulders. A vast red blister swelled visibly from his patchy hairline almost to the soiled edge of the underwear showing above his belt. His eye fell on Doc.

"Do something, damn your guts!" he shrilled. "Oh, Jesus . . ."

Doc started around the table. I caught his arm. "To hell with that sadist," I said. "Take a look at Joel's hands."

Joel still stood, staring at his hands. A tear formed, rolled down his cheek.

"I'll kill him!" Pogey screeched. He plunged across the room, knocked the sailor aside, caught up a steak knife, and whirled on Joel. I pushed in front of him. The odors of sweat and alcohol came from him in waves. I caught his wrist, remembering not to pulp the bone.

"Joel," I said, my eyes holding on Pogey's. "If this man ever hurts you again, put your thumbs into his throat until he stops moving, understand?"

I twitched the knife from Pogey's hand, shoved him away. His face was as white as the dead face of the thing I had killed in the ravine. The recollection must have shown in my expression.

Pogey whimpered, backed, turned to the sailor who was standing wide-eyed, all warts and Adam's apple, looking from one of us to another like a spectator at a ping-pong tournament.

"Get me to my room," Pogey gasped. His knees went slack as the sailor caught him. Behind me, Joel moaned.

"Let's get this boy down to my sick-bay," Doc was saying. "Second-degree, maybe worse. Calluses helped . . ."

As I turned, his eyes found mine. "You better let

me take a look at you, too," he said. "You're hotter'n a power pile, Jones."

"Never mind that," I snapped. "Just see to Joel."

Doc eyed the cut on my face. "You should have had a couple of stitches."

"All I need is to get to Jax and get clear of this scow," I said. "Let's get moving."

Doc shrugged. "Suit yourself." He went out, leading Joel. I followed.

An hour later, in the cramped, paper-heaped room the Mate called his office, I stood before the ancient plastic-topped desk, waiting for him to finish his tirade. Two sailors lounged against the wall, watching. Joel stood beside me, his bandage-swathed hands looking bigger than ever. Carboni's good eye looked up at him from under his ragged eyebrows.

"I had enough of your numbskull tricks," he growled. "When we hit Jax, you're finished."

"Gosh, Carboni," Joel started.

"Beat it," the Mate said. "I got work to do." He switched his glance to me. "You stick around, I got things to say to you."

I put a hand on the desk to keep it from spinning.

"How's Pogey feeling?" My voice seemed to belong to someone else.

Carboni's meaty face darkened.

"We'll see about you when we hit Jax, punk. I got plans for you."

"Don't bother," I said. "I intend to resign my position anyway."

"I'm a patient guy." Carboni got to his feet, walked around the desk. "But I got a bellyfull—" He pivoted suddenly, threw a punch that slammed against my stomach. He jumped back with a bellow, his face draining to a dirty white. One of the sailors brought a hand into view behind him, pointed a massive, old-model blued-steel Browning needle-gun at my belt buckle.

We waited, not moving, while Carboni cursed, gripping his fist and grinding his plates.

"Walk him to the brig, Slocum!" he roared. "And watch him! There's something funny about this guy!"

The gun-handler jabbed the weapon at me. "Get moving, you."

The brig was a bare-walled cell illuminated by a single overhead glare panel and outfitted with a stainless-steel water closet with stains, and a hinged plastic shelf two feet wide padded with a mouldy smelling matresss half an inch thick.

I sat on the floor, leaned against the wall; the feel of the cool metal was soothing to my hot face. The beat of my pulse was like a brass gong behind my temples. My left forearm ached to the shoulder with a deep-seated pain that made every movement an ordeal. I turned the sleeve back; under the crude dressing, the wounds were inflamed, evil-looking.

I got out a tube of ointment Doc had given me, applied it to the ragged cuts, smeared more on the slash across my face, managed to reach the higher of the wounds on my left shoulder before the supply ran out.

A panel covering a peephole in the door clanged open. A pale, fat man with a crumpled white-billed cap peered in at me through the foot-square grille. He muttered and turned away. I keened my hearing, followed him:

"... dock at Jacksonville ... nine hours ..."

"... in touch with 'em ..." Carboni's voice said, fading now as they moved away. "... in irons ... on the pier ..."

"... don't like it ... ask questions ..."

I sat up, fighting against a throbbing fever-daze in which the events of the past weeks mingled with fragments of nightmare. Jacksonville in nine hours, the Captain had said. It was time to start planning.

I got to my feet, swaying like a palm-tree in a high wind. I went to the door, ignoring violent pains in my skull. I pushed against the door, gauging its strength. It was solid, massively hinged, and with a locking bar engaged at both ends, impossible to force, even if I hadn't been weakened by fever.

I went back, wavered as I walked, and half-fell to the floor. A wave of nausea rolled over me, and left me shivering violently.

I would have to wait ... I forced my thoughts to hold to the subject. *Wait until they came to open the cell door. There would be a band, dressed all in red, and General Julius would be leading it* ...

I fought the fantasy away. Delirium waited like a mire beside the narrow path of reason. *Nothing to do with Julius. Julius was dead. I had strangled him, while he bit at me. The dog-things had chased me, and now I was on the beach. It was cold, cold* ... I shivered violently, huddling against the steel cliff ...

Time passed, Joel was calling my name. He needed help, but I was trapped here. There was a way up the cliff: I could fly. I had the suit, and now I was fitting the helmet in place, and through it, Joel stared with agony-filled eyes—

There were hands on me, voices near. A sharp pain stabbed in my arm. I pulled away, fighting a weight that crushed me.

"Please, Jones ... don't hit the Doc ..."

I got my eyes open. Joel's face loomed above me. Blood ran from his nose. Doc's frightened face stared. I fell back, feeling my heart pound like a shoeing hammer.

"Can you hold him, boy?" Doc's voice was anxious.

"S'all righ'," I managed. "Awake now . . ."

"You been awful sick, Jones," Joel said. He raised his bandaged hand, dabbed at his nose, smeared blood across his cheek. Doc moved closer, working over me. I felt his hands on my arm. He grunted.

"My God, Jones, what did this?"

"Dog-bite." My voice was a hoarse whisper.

"Another few hours . . . no attention . . . burial at sea . . ." his voice came and went. I fought to hold onto consciousness.

". . . can't get a hypospray to penetrate," he was saying. "Damnedest thing I ever saw. Can you swallow this?"

I sat up, gulped something icy cold. Doc's eyes bored into mine.

"I've given you something to fight the infection," he said. "It ought to bring the fever down, too. That arm's bad, Jones. It may have to come off."

I laughed—a crazy, high-pitched giggle that rolled on and on.

Doc's face was closer now. "I never saw anything like this before," he said. "I ought to report it to the Skipper—"

I stopped laughing; my hand went out, caught at his coat-front.

"I heard some of what you said when you were raving," Doc went on. "I don't claim to understand— but I know you for a decent man. I don't know what to think. But I wouldn't throw a sick dog to Carboni. I won't tell 'em."

"S'all right," I croaked. "Go' job do . . . go' ge' well. Fix me up, Doc . . ."

"I've got to work on the arm now. Try to relax."

I lay back and let the dream take me.

I awoke feeling weak, sick, beaten, thrown away. I stirred, heard cloth tear. I looked down; my left arm, as numb as something carved from marble, was strapped to my side. I felt the pull of tape at my neck, across my jaw. My mouth tasted as though mice had nested in it. I sat up. I was as weak as a diplomatic protest.

I got to my feet, blinked away a light-shot blackness, went across to the door, and looked out through the bars. Joel lay in the corridor, asleep on a mat. I called his name.

He sat up, rubbed his eyes, smiled.

"Hey, Jones!" He got to his feet, touched his swollen nose. "Boy, Jones, you sure pack a wallop. You feeling better now?"

"Lots better. How long was I out?"

He looked down at me vaguely.

"How long before we reach Jacksonville?"

"Gosh, Jones, I dunno. Pretty soon, maybe."

I tensed the muscles behind my ears, tuned through the sounds of the ship, picked up the mutter of voices; but they were indistinct, unreadable.

"Listen, Joel. You heard what Carboni said. There'll be police waiting for me when we dock. I have to get off the ship before then. How long before we surface?"

"Huh? Hey, how come the cops is after you, Jones?"

"Never mind that. Try to think, now: do we surface out at sea, before we get into the harbor?"

Joel frowned. "Gosh, I don't know about that, Jones."

I gripped the bars. "I've got to know what time it is—where we are."

"Uh . . ."

"I want you to do something for me, Joel. Go to the crew mess. There's a clock there. Go check it, and come back and tell me what time it is."

Joel nodded. "Okay, Jones. Sure. How come—"

"I'll tell you later. Hurry."

I sat on the floor and waited. The deck seemed

to surge under me. Either we were maneuvering, or I was getting ready to have another relapse.

There was a distant booming, the sudden vibration of turbulence transmitted through the hull. The ship heaved, settled. I got to my feet, holding to the wall for support.

There were sounds along the corridor: the clump of feet, raised voices. I keened my hearing again, picked up the whine of the main-drive turbines, the clatter of deploying deck gear, the creak of the hull—and another sound: the rhythmic growl of a small-boat engine, far away but coming closer.

The minutes crawled by like stepped-on roaches. Joel appeared down the corridor, came up to the cell door. There was a worried look on his face. "The big hand was . . . le'ssee . . . Hey, Jones . . ." He looked at me like a lost kid. "I got a funny feeling—"

"Sure, Joel. I'm scared, too."

"But I got this like tickle-feeling in my head."

I nodded absently, listening for the sounds from above. The boat was close now; I heard its engines cut back, then it was bumping alongside. The sound of the ship's turbines had faded to a growl.

"Does a Customs boat usually come out to meet the ship in the harbor?" Joel was rubbing his head with one bandaged hand. He looked up at the low ceiling and whimpered.

"What is it, Joel?" Then I felt it: the eerie sense of unreality, the graying of the light in the dim corridor, the sense of doom. I grabbed the bars, strained at them. The metal gave, grudgingly, a fraction of an inch. My head pounded from the effort.

"Joel!" I called. My voice had a ragged edge. "Who keeps the key to this door?"

His eyes wavered down to meet mine. "Jones— I'm scared."

"I need the key, Joel." I tried to keep my voice calm. "Who has it?"

"Uh—Carboni. He keeps all the keys."

"Can you get them?"

Joel looked at the ceiling. I heard feet on the deck now—and a soft padding that sent a chill through me like an iron spear.

"Joel—I need those keys. I've got to get out of here!"

He came close to the door, pressing against it. His eyes were sick. "I got such a tickle in my head," he moaned. "I'm scared, Jones."

"Don't be afraid." I gripped his hand that clutched one of the bars.

"Sometimes—" he brushed at his face, groping for words. "When I see the big dogs— It was just like this, Jones; it tickled in my head."

I swallowed hard. "Tell me about the big dogs, Joel."

"I didn't like them dogs, Jones. They scared me. I run when I seen 'em. I hid."

"When did you see them?"

"In port. Lots of times. I seen 'em in the streets, and inside buildings. I seen 'em looking out of cars." He pointed to the ceiling. "They're up there now; I can tell."

"Listen, Joel. Go to Carboni's office; get the keys; the one you want is a big electrokey. Bring it here, as fast as you can."

"I'm scared, Jones."

"Hurry—before they come down below decks!"

Joel stepped back with a sob, turned, and ran. I clung to the bars and waited, listening to the feet that prowled the deck above.

The ship was deathly still except for the slap of water, the groan of structural members as the hull flexed under the motion of the waves. I heard stealthy feet moving, the rasp of unhuman hands at the deckhouse door.

Far away, Joel's footsteps moved uncertainly,

hurrying a few steps, then pausing. Nearer, there
was a creak of unoiled hinges; then soft footsteps
moved down the forward companionway. I tried
the bars again. The fever had drained my strength
as effectively as a slashed artery.

Joel's solid, human footsteps were coming back
now; the other feet paced a cross-corridor, coming
closer, crossing an intersection fifty feet away, going
on . . .

Joel appeared, half-running. I heard the other
footsteps slow, come to a stop. I pictured the thing,
standing with one pale hand upraised like a dog
on point, its death-mask turning, searching.

I motioned to Joel. "Keep it quiet!" I whispered.
He came up to the door, holding the key, a two-
inch square of black plastic from which a short
metal rod protruded.

"Carboni was setting right there; he never even
looked up."

"Get the door open."

He inserted the key, his tongue in the corner of
his mouth. I could hear the thing around the corner, coming back now, hurrying. The lock snicked;
I slid the door aside, stepped into the passage.

The creature bounded into view, brought up
short, red eyes staring in a white mask. Beside me,
Joel cried out. I pushed in front of him as the
demon sprang. I slammed a blow to its head that
sent it sprawling past me. It was up instantly,
whirling, rearing up on thin, too-long legs. I
chopped at its neck with the side of my hand,
jumped back as its jaws snapped half an inch from
my wrist. Its hands were on me, groping for my
throat. I jerked free, swung a kick that caught its
hip, knocked it against the wall. It yelped, came at
me, dragging a hind leg. Behind it, Joel stood,
mouth open, flat against the cell door.

I shook my head to clear it. The scene before me

was wavering; a sound like roaring waters filled my head . . .

A cannonball struck me, carried me back, down. The needle-filled mouth was a foot from my face, and I hit at it, felt bone crunch under my fist. I struck again, twisted aside from a snarling lunge, caught a fistful of stiff-bristled hide, held the snapping jaws away. The great pale hands struck at me—poorly aimed, feeble blows; the jaws were the demon's weapon. They ravened inches from my face—and my arm was weakening . . .

The beast lunged backward, twisted free from my one-handed grip. I heard Joel's yell, instantly choked off. I came to my knees, saw the flurry of motion as the demon bore him backwards.

I got my feet under me, took two steps, threw myself at the black-bristled back. I locked my right arm around its throat in a crushing embrace. I lunged backward, rolled clear of Joel, saw him stumble to his feet, start toward me—

"Stay clear!" I shouted. The demon fought, flailing the deck and walls with wild blows of its four hands. I held on, choking it, feeling bone and cartilage collapse, grinding the shattered throat until the head fell slack. One leg drummed for a moment against the deck; then the thing stiffened and was still.

I pushed it aside, tottered to my feet. Joel stared at me, dazed. I listened, heard the slap of running beast-hands.

"Into the cell, Joel—" I pushed him inside, slammed and locked the door.

"You'll be safe there—they won't bother with you," I called. "When you get ashore, go home, stay there. No matter what—stay in Jacksonville. You understand?"

He nodded dumbly. The feet were close now.

I turned, ran along the passage, took a cross-corridor, nearly fell over Runt, lying sprawled on

the deck. A patch of evening sky showed at the top
of the companionway. I went up, leaped out on the
open deck, almost awash in the still sea. I caught a
glimpse of two demons standing with raised heads,
listening, while beyond them a third crouched over
a fallen crewman. Three steps took me to the rail;
I leaped over it and dived into the dark water.

I came to shore in a tangle of water hyacinth
rooted in the soft mud of a river's edge. For a long
time I lay flat on my face, waiting for the sickness
to drain away. There were far-off sounds of life:
the rumble of a monorail, the hoot of a tug out in
the harbor. Nearer, a dog barked. Mosquitoes
whined insistently.

I turned on my back. Giant stars blazed across a
sky like charred velvet. The air was hot, heavy,
oppressive. There was an odor of river muck and
decayed vegetation. I got to my feet, staggering a
little. I waded out, washed the mud off me. The
bandages were sodden weights; I removed them,
splashed water on the wounds. The left arm worried me; even in the near-total darkness I could see
that it was grossly swollen, the cuts gaping wide.
It was not so painful now, though; whatever Doc
had given me was doing its work.

I turned and made my way to higher ground. A
sandy road cut across the edge of a planted field
before me, a strip of lesser black against the darkness. I squinted, trying to bring my night-vision
into play. For a moment the scene flicked from
black to gray; then pain clamped on my head like
a vise. I gave it up.

A light was shining through moss-laden live oaks
in the distance. I started off, stumbling in the
loose sand. Once I fell, slammed my face hard. I
lay for minutes, spitting sand feebly and trying
out some of Carboni's Sicilian curses. They seemed
to help. After a while I got up and went on.

*　　*　　*

It was a cabin sided with corrugated aluminum panels, a sagging structure supported mainly by a towering Tri-D antenna. A gleaming, late-model Mercette ground car stood in the yard. I crept up to it, glanced in, saw the glint of keys in the starter switch.

The light in the house came from an unshaded glare-lamp on a table by the window. I saw a tall man cross the room, come back a moment later with a glass in his hand. He seemed to be the only one in the house.

I studied the lay of the land. The ungrassed yard slanted down to the edge of the road, which ran level into the darkness. I opened the driver's door carefully, checked the brake, released it. A slight push started the car rolling backwards. I padded beside it, guiding it for the first few yards; then I slid into the seat, cut the wheel, rolled out onto the road. I switched on, let out the clutch; I moved off with the engine purring as softly as a spoon stirring thick cream.

I looked back; the cabin was peaceful. There would be a bad scene when the car was missed, but an anonymous cashier's check would remedy the pain.

Coffeyville, Kansas, Felix had said. Box 1742, the Franklin Street Postal Station. It was a long drive for an invalid, and what I would find at the end of it I didn't know—but it was something that Felix had thought important enough to lock in the final strongbox in his subconscious.

I drove slowly for half a mile, then switched on my lights, swung into a paved highway, and headed north.

Chapter Nine

I followed secondary roads, skirting towns, driving at a carefully legal speed. At the first light of dawn I pulled into a run-down motel near the Georgia line with a wan glare sign indicating VAC NCY. From behind a screened door, an aging woman in a dirty housecoat and curlers blinked eyes like burned-out coals nested in putty-colored wrinkles.

"Take number six," she whined. "That's ten cees—in advance, seein's you got no luggage." A hand like a croupier's rake poked the key at me, accepted payment.

I pulled the car under the overhang, as nearly out of sight from the road as possible. I crossed a cracked concrete porch, and stepped into a stifling hot room as slatternly as its owner. In the stale-smelling dark, I pulled off my coat, found the bath cubicle, splashed cold water on my face at the orange-stained china sink. I dried myself on a stiff towel the size of a place-mat.

I showered and washed out my clothes, hung

them on the curtain rail, and stretched out on the hard mattress. My fever was still high. I dozed fitfully for a few hours, went through a seizure of chills followed by violent nausea.

Late in the afternoon I took a second shower, dressed in my stained but dry clothes, and went across the highway to the Paradise Eat, an adobe-like rectangle of peeling light-blue paint crusted with beer signs.

A thin girl with hollow eyes stared at me, silently served me leathery pancakes with watered syrup and a massive mug of boiled coffee, then sat on a stool as far from me as possible and used a toothpick. Her eyes ran over me like mice.

I finished and offered her a five-cee bill. "How's the road to Jackson?" I asked, more to find out if she had a voice than anything else. It didn't work. She looked at me suspiciously, handed over my change, went back to her stool.

Back across the road, I started the car up, pulled across to the one-pump service station. A heavy-bellied, sly-faced man in a coverall filled the tank, looking the car over.

"Goin' far?" he inquired.

"Just up Bogalusa way," I said.

He studied the pump gauge, topped off, clamped the cap in place. He seemed to take a long time about it.

"How's 'at transmission fluid?" he asked. His eyes slipped past mine; heavy-lidded eyes, as guileless as a stud dealer with aces wired.

I handed him his money, added a cee note. "Better check it."

He pocketed the money, made a production of lifting the access panel, wiping the stick, squinting at it.

"Full up," he allowed. He replaced the stick, closed the panel. "Nice car," he said. "How long since you been in Bogalusa?"

"Quite a time," I said. "I've been overseas."

"Plant closed down a year ago," he said. "If you was looking for work." He cocked his head, studying my arm. His expression was shrewdly complacent now, like a clever dealer about to get his price.

"You in one of them wars?" he inquired.

"I fell off a bar-stool."

He shot me a look like a knife-thrust.

"Just tryin' to be friendly . . ." His gaze went to the call-screen inside the station. He took a tire gauge from a breast pocket. "Better check them tars," he grunted.

"Never mind; they're okay."

He walked past me to the front of the car, lifted the inspection plate, reached in, and plucked the power fuse from its base.

"What are you doing?"

"Better check this here out, too." He went across to the station. I followed him; he was whistling uneasily, watching me from the corner of an eye. I went over to the screen, got a good grip on the power lead, and yanked it from the back of the set.

He yelled, dived for the counter, came up with a tire iron. I stepped aside, caught his arm, slammed him against the wall. The iron clanged to the floor. I hauled him to a chair and threw him into it.

"The fuse," I snapped.

"Over there." He jerked his head sulleny.

"Don't get up." I went behind the counter, recovered the fuse.

"Who were you going to call?"

He began to bluster. I kicked him in the shin, gently. He howled.

"I don't have time to waste," I snapped. "The whole story—fast!"

"They's a call out on you," he bleated. "I seen the tag number soon's I went around back to cap up. You won't get far."

"Why not?"

He stared at me, slumped in the chair. I kicked the other leg. "Sheriff's got a road-block two, three miles north," he yelped.

"How good a description?"

"Said you had a bad arm, scar on your face; 'scribed them clothes, too." He pulled himself up. "You ain't got a chance, mister."

I went over and picked up a roll of friction tape from the counter, came back and pulled him to his feet, reached for his arms. He tugged against me feebly; his mouth was suddenly loose with fear.

"Here, what are you gonna—"

"I haven't decided yet. It depends on your cooperation." I set to work taping his hands behind him. "What's the best way around the road-block?"

"Looky here, mister, you want to slip past that road-block, you just take your next left, half a mile up the road . . ." He was babbling in his eagerness to please. "Hell, they'll never figger you to know about that. Jist a farm road. Comes out at Reform, twelve mile west."

I finished trussing him, looked around the room; there was a smudged, white-painted door marked MEN. Inside, I found soap and water on the shelf above a black-ringed bowl. I took five minutes to run the electroshave over my face.

There were plastic bandages in a small box in the cabinet; I covered the cut along my jaw as well as I could, then combed my hair back. I looked better now—like someone who'd been hurriedly worked over by a bargain mortician, rather than just a corpse carelessly thrown into a ditch.

I dragged the owner into the john, left him on the floor, taped and gagged; I hung the CLOSED sign on the outer door and shut it behind me.

There was a mud-spattered pickup parked beside the station. The fuel gauge read full. I drove my Mercette onto the grease rack, ran it up high.

There was a blue Navy weather jacket, not too dirty, hanging by the rack. I put it on, leaving the bad arm out of the sleeve. I waited a moment for the dizziness to pass, then climbed into the pickup and eased out onto the highway, ignoring the nagging feeling that hidden eyes were watching.

The night was a bad dream without an end; hour after hour of droning tires, the whine of the turbine, the highway unwinding out of darkness while I clung to the wheel, fighting off the cycle of fever blackout, nausea, chills, and fever again.

Just before dawn, ten miles south of the Oklahoma-Kansas border, a police cruiser pulled in alongside me as I swung the wide curve of an intermix. A cop with coldly handome features and soot-black eyes looked me over expressionlessly. I gave him a foolish grin, waved, then slowed; the cruiser gunned ahead, swung off onto the expressway.

I reduced speed, turned off on the first single-lane track I saw, bumped along past decaying farmhouses and collapsed barns for six miles, then pulled back onto my route at a town called Cherokee Farm. There were lights on in the Transport Café. I parked, went in, and took a corner table with a view of the door, and ordered hot cereal. I ate it slowly, concentrating on keeping it down. My head was getting bad again, and the pain in my wooden arm made my teeth ache. I was traveling on raw nerve-power and drugs now; without the artificial reservoir of strength that my PAPA gear gave me, I would have collapsed hours before.

As it was, I was able to peer through the film of gray that hung before my eyes, swallow the food mechanically, walk to the cashier without excessive wavering, pay up, and go back out into the icy night to my pickup, with no more inconvenience

than a sensation of deathly illness and a nagging
fear that I was dreaming everything.

An hour later, I steered the pickup to the curb
on a snow-frosted side street of sagging, cavernous
houses that had been the culminating achievements
of rich farmers a century before. Now they looked
as bleak and empty as abandoned funeral homes.

I got out of the car, waited until the pavement
settled down, then walked back two blocks to a
structure in red-brick Gothic bearing the legend:

RAILROAD MENS YMCA
Coffeyville, Kansas, 1965

Inside, a bored-looking youngish man with thinning hair and a pursed mouth watched me from
behind the peeling veneer of a kidney-shaped desk
with a faded sign reading: WELCOME BROTHER,
and another, hand-lettered, announcing: SHOWER—
FIFTY DOLLARS.

I ignored the sea of gray jello in which his face
seemed to float, got a hand on the desk, leaned
more or less upright, and heard somebody say,
"I'd like a room for tonight."

His mouth was moving. It was hot in the room. I
pulled at my collar. The jello had closed over the
clerk now, but a voice with an edge like a meat-
saw went on:

". . . drunks in the place. You'll have to clear out
of here. This is a Christian organization."

"Unfortunately, I'm not drunk." I heard myself
pronouncing the words quite distinctly. "I'm a bit
off my feed; touch of an old malaria, possibly . . ."

He was swimming back into focus. My feet
seemed to be swinging in a slow arc over my head.
I kept both hands on the counter and tried to
convince myself that I was standing solidly on the
rubber mat that covered the worn place in the rug.
I let go long enough to get out my wallet, put
money on the counter.

"Well . . ." His hand covered the bill. "You do look a little flushed. Chinese flu, maybe. Maybe you'd better see a doctor. And that's a nasty cut on your face."

"Not used to these new-fangled safety razors," I said. "I'll be all right." The floor was sliding back to where it belonged. The jello had thinned out sufficiently to show me the registration book and a finger with a hangnail indicating where I should sign.

My stomach felt like a flush tank on the verge of starting its cycle. I grabbed the stylus, scrawled something, waded through knee-deep fog to the lift. I rode up, walked past a few miles of wallpaper that was someone's revenge for life's disappointments. I found my room, got the door open, took a step toward the bed, and passed out cold.

A crew of little red men was working at my arm with saws and hatchets, while another played a blowtorch over my face. I tried to yell to scare them away, and managed a weak croak. I got my eyes open, discovered that my face was against a dusty rug with a pattern of faded fruits and flowers.

I crawled as far as the wall-mounted lavatory, pulled myself up, got the cold water on, and splashed it over my head. I could hear myself moaning, like a dog begging to be let in on a cold night; it didn't seem important.

There was yellow light outside the dirt-scaled window when I tottered across to the bed. The next time I looked, it was deep twilight. Time seemed to be slipping by in large pieces, like an ice-floe breaking up. I got up on the third try, went back, and used some more cold water, then braced my feet and risked a look in the mirror. A gray-white mask with a quarter-inch beard stared at me with red, crusted eyes buried in blue-black hollows. The scars across my nose and beside my mouth from Felix's plastic surgery were vivid slashes of red. Under the curled plastic tapes, the cut along my jaw showed deep and ragged.

I made it back to the bed and fumbled out my wallet; I still had plenty of money. Now was the time to use some. I punched the screen's audio circuit, signaled the desk. The clerk came on, sounding irritated.

"Is there an all-night autoshop in town?" I asked, trying to sound sober, sincere, and financially reliable.

"Certainly. Two of them."

"Good. I'll pay someone five cees to pick up a few things for me."

In two minutes he was at my door. I handed through the list I had scribbled, along with a bundle of money.

"Yes, *sir!*" he said. "Won't take half an hour. Ah . . . sure you don't want me to fetch a doctor?"

"Christian Scientist," I mumbled. He went away, and I sprawled out on the bed to wait.

An hour later, with half a dozen assorted antipyretics, cortical stimulants, metabolic catalyzers, and happy pills in my stomach, I took a hot shower, shaved, put a clean tape on my jaw, and worked my arm into my new olive-drab one-piece suit. I pocketed my other supplies and went downstairs. I didn't feel much better, but the clerk nodded happily when I came up to the desk; I gathered that I now looked more like what you'd expect to find in a Christian organization.

"Ah—the nut-hammer," he said, not quite looking at me. "Was it what you had in mind?"

"Ideal," I said. "They just don't taste the same unless you crack 'em yourself, the old-fashioned way."

He used his worried look on me.

"Maybe you hadn't ought to go out, sir," he

suggested. "All those medicines you had me buy—they're just pain-killers—"

"My pains aren't dead—just wounded," I assured him. He gave me the blank look my kind of wisecrack usually nets. "By the way," I ploughed on, "where's Franklin Street?"

He gave me directions, and I went out into the chill of the late autumn night. I considered calling a cab, but decided against it. My experiences had made me wary of sharing confined spaces with strangers. Using the pickup was out, too; a hot car might attract just the attention I didn't want at the moment.

I started off at a wobbling gait that steadied as the chemicals in my bloodstream started to work. My breath was freezing into ice-crystals in the bitter air. The route the clerk had given me led me gradually toward brighter-lit streets. I scanned the people on the sidewalks for signs of interest in me; they seemed normal enough.

I spotted the post office from half a block away; it had a low, yellowish armorplast front with a glass door flanked on one side by a code-punch panel, and on the other by colorful exhortations to 'Enlist Now in the Peace Brigade and Fight for the Way of Life of Your Choice.'

I strolled on past to get the lay of the land, went on as far as the corner, then turned and came back at a medium-brisk pace. My medication was doing its job; I felt like something specially snipped out of sheet metal for the occasion: bright, and with plenty of sharp edges, but not too hard to punch a hole through.

I stopped in front of the panel, punched keys one, seven, four, and two. Machinery whirred. A box popped into view. Through the quarter-inch armorplast, I could see a thick manila envelope. The proper code would cause the transparent panel

to slide up—but unfortunately Felix hadn't had time
to give it to me.

I took another look both ways, lifted the nut-
hammer from my pocket, and slammed it against
the plastic. It made a hell of a loud noise; a faint
mark appeared on the panel. I set myself, hit it
again as hard as I could. The plastic shattered. I
poked the sharp fragments in, got my fingers on
the envelope, pulled it out through the jagged opening. I could hear a bell starting up inside the building. Nearer at hand, a red light above the door
blinked furiously. It was unfortunate—but a risk I
had had to take. I tucked the envelope away, turned,
took two steps—

A loping dog-shape rounded the corner, galloped
silently toward me. I turned; a second was angling
across the street at a dead run. Far down the
street, two pedestrians sauntered on their ways,
oblivious of what was happening. There was no
one else in sight. A third demon appeared at an
alley mouth across the street, trotted directly
toward me, sharp ears erect, skull-face smiling.

There was a dark delivery-van at the curb. I
leaped to it, tried the door—locked. I doubled my
fist, smashed the glass, got the door open. The
nearest demon broke into an awkward gallop.

I slid into the seat, twisted the key, accelerated
from the curb as the thing leaped. It struck just
behind the door, clung for a moment, and fell off. I
steered for the one in the street ahead, saw it
dodge aside at the last instant—just too late. There
was a heavy shock; the car veered. I caught it,
rounded a corner on two wheels, steering awkwardly with one hand. The gyros screeched their
protest as I zigzagged, missed another dog-thing
coming up fast, then straightened out and roared
off along the street, past stores, a service station,
houses, then open fields. Blood was running from
my knuckles, trickling under my sleeve.

There was a clump of dark trees ahead, growing down almost to the edge of the road. A little farther on, the polyarcs of a major expressway intermix gleamed across the dark prairie. I caught a glimpse of a roadside sign:

CAUTION—KANSAS 199—¼ MI.
SW. AUTODRIVE 100 YDS.
MANDATORY ABOVE 100 MPH

I braked quickly, passed the blue glare sign that indicated the pickup point for the state autodrive system, squealed to a stop fifty yards beyond it. I switched the drive lever to AUTO, set the cruise control on MAXLEG., jumped out, reached back in to flick the van into gear. It started off, came quickly up to speed, jerkily corrected course as it crossed the system monitor line. I watched it as it swung off into the banked curve ahead, accelerating rapidly; then I climbed an ancient wire fence, stumbled across a snow-scattered ploughed field and into the shelter of the trees.

Excitement, I was discovering wasn't good for my ailment. I had another attack of nausea that left me pale, trembling, empty as a looted house, and easily strong enough to sort out a stamp collection. I swayed on all fours, smelling leaf-mold and frozen bark, hearing a distant croak of treefrogs, the faraway wail of a horn.

The demons had laid a neat trap for me. They had watched, followed my movements—probably from the time I left the ship—waiting for the time to close in. For the moment, I had confused them. For all their power, they seemed to lack the ability to counter the unexpected—the human ability to improvise in an emergency, to act on impulse.

My trick with the van had gained me a few minutes' respite—but nothing more. Alerted police would bring the empty vehicle to halt within a mile or two; then a cordon would close in, beating every thicket, until they found me.

Meanwhile, I had time enough to take a look at whatever it was that I had come five thousand miles to collect—the thing Felix had guarded with the last fragment of his will. I took the envelope from an inner pocket, tore off one end. A two-inch-square wafer of translucent polyon slipped into my hand. In the faint starlight, I could see a pattern of fine wires and vari-colored beads embedded in the material. I turned it over, smelled it, shook it, held it to my ear—

"Identify yourself," a tiny voice said.

I jumped, held the thing on my palm to stare at it, then cautiously put it to my ear again.

"You now have sixty seconds in which to identify yourself," the voice said. *"Fifty-eight seconds and counting . . ."*

I held the rectangle to my mouth.

"Bravais," I said. "John Bravais, CBI SA-0654."

I listened again:

". . . fifty-two; fifty-one; fifty . . ."

I talked to it some more.

". . . forty-four; forty-three; forty-two . . ."

Talking to it wasn't getting me anywhere. How the hell did you identify yourself to a piece of plastic the size of a book of matches? Fingerprints? A National Geographic Society membership card?

I pulled out my CBI card, held it to the plastic, then listened again:

". . . thirty-one; thirty . . ." There was a pause. *"In the absence of proper identification within thirty seconds, this plaque will detonate. Unauthorized personnel are warned to withdraw to fifty yards. . . . Twenty seconds and counting. Nineteen; eighteen . . ."*

I had my arm back, ready to throw. I checked the motion. The blast would attract everything within a mile, from flying saucer watchers to red-eyed beast-shapes that loped on hands like a man's, and I would have lost my one ace in a game where the stakes were more than life and death.... I hesitated, looked at the ticking bomb in my hand. "Thinking caps, children," I whispered aloud. "Thinking caps, thinking caps . . ."

Talking to it was no good. ID cards with built-in molecular patterns for special scanners meant nothing to it. It had to be something simple, something Felix hadn't had time to tell me . . .

A signal had to be transmitted. I had nothing—except an array of gimmicks built into my teeth by Felix—

There was a spy-eye detector that would set up a sharp twinge in my left upper canine under any radiation on the spy band; the right lower incisor housed a CBI emergency band receiver; in my right lower third molar, there was a miniature radar pulser—

A transmitter. Just possibly—if there was still time. I jammed the plaque to my ear:

". . . *ten seconds and counting. Nine*—"

With my tongue, I pushed aside the protective cap on the tooth, bit down. There was a sour taste of galvanic action as the contacts closed, a tingle as an echo bounced back from metal somewhere out across the night. I pulsed again; if that hadn't done it, nothing would.

I cocked my arm to throw the thing—

But if I did—and it failed to explode—I would never find it again in the dark, not in time. And it was too late to drop it and run . . . not that I had anything left to run with. I gritted my teeth, held the thing to my head . . .

". . . *two* . . ." The pause seemed to go on and on.

"*You are recognized*," the voice said crisply. "*You are now seven hundred and thirty-two yards north-north-east of the station*."

I felt a pang of emotion in which relief and

regret mingled. Now the chase would go on; there would be no rest for me. Not yet . . .

I got to my feet, took a bearing on the north star, and set off through the trees.

I came out of the woods onto an unsurfaced track, went through a ditch choked with stiff, waist-high weeds, scraped myself getting over a rotting wire fence. There were headlights on the highway now, swinging off onto the side road, and other lights coming out from Coffeyville. The patch of woods would be the obvious first place to search. In another five minutes, the hunters would be emerging on the spot where I now stood ankle-deep in the clods of a stubbled cornfield. I couldn't tell what was on the far side; my night vision was long gone. I broke into a shambling run, across the frozen furrows, tripping at every third step, falling often. The thudding of my heart was almost drowned by the roaring in my head.

Something low and dark lay across my path—the ruins of a row of sheds. I angled off to skirt them, and slammed full-tilt into a fence, sending fragments of rotted wood flying as I sprawled. I sat up, put the wafer to my ear.

". . . *six hundred twenty-two yards, bearing two-oh-seven,*" the calm voice said. I struggled up, picked my way past the rusted hulk of a tractor abandoned under the crabbed branches of a dead apple tree. I came back into the open, broke into a run across a grassy stretch that had probably been a pasture forty years earlier. Faint light fell across the ground ahead; my shadow bobbed, swung aside, and disappeared. Cars were maneuvering, closing in on the woodlot behind me. Fence posts loomed up ahead; I slowed, jumped a tangle of fallen wires, ran on across another field, plowed by the auto-tillers months before but never planted.

The suffocating sensation of oxygen starvation

burned in my chest; I hadn't thought to charge my
storage units. I drew a long painful breath, brought
the plastic rectangle up to my head as I ran.

"... *yards, bearing two one two ... four hundred
and fifty-four yards, bearing two one three ...*"

I corrected course to the right, plunged down a
slight slope, crashed through a dense growth of
brush, went knee-deep into half-frozen muck, sending skim-ice tinkling. Dry stalks broke under my
hand as I clawed my way up an embankment;
then I was up again, running with feet that seemed
to be cased in concrete.

A dirt road crossed my path ahead at a slight
angle. I leaped a ditch, followed the track as it
curved, and crossed another. A grove of massive
dark trees came into view well off to my right—
century-old patriarchs, standing alone. I came to a
gasping halt, listened to check my position: "...
*one hundred eighteen yards, bearing two seven five
...*" I left the road, ran for the distant trees.

A tall frame house with a collapsed roof leaned
in the shelter of the grove. Vacant windows looked
blindly out across the dark field. I went past it,
past a fallen barn, the remains of outbuildings.
"... *one yard, bearing two five two ...*"

And there was nothing; not so much as a marker
stone or a dry bush. Standing alone in the frozen
field, shivering now with the bitter cold, I could
hear the approaching feet clearly now—more than
one set of them.

I turned to face them, taking deep breaths to
charge my air banks. I tried to blink the fog from
my eyes. It would be over in another minute; I
would try to kill at least one more of them before
those bony snouts found my throat. . . .

I started to toss the useless plaque aside, but on
impulse put it to my ear instead.

"—*rectly above the entry; please re-identify. . . .*

You are now directly above the entry; please re-identify. . . . You are now—"

I groped with my tongue, bit down on the tooth. Nothing happened. Through the darkness, I saw a movement among the scattered trees. Near at hand, there was a soft hum, a grating sound. Directly before me, dirt stirred; a polished cylinder a yard across, dirt-topped, emerged from the earth, rose swiftly to a height of six feet. With a *click!* a panel slid back, exposing an unlighted and featureless interior. I stepped inside. The panel slid shut. I felt the cylinder start down. It sank, sank, slowed, halted. I leaned against the curving wall, fighting off the dizziness. The panel slid aside; and I stumbled out into warmth and silence.

Chapter Ten

I was in a small, softly-lit room with a polished floor, warm to the touch, and walls that were a jumble of ancient, varnished oak cabinet-work, gray-painted equipment housings, instrument panels, indicator lights, and controls resembling those of a Tri-D starship. Exposed wiring and conduit criss-crossed the panels; a vast wall clock with fanciful roman numerals and elaborate hands said ten minutes past ten. There was a faint hum of recycling air. I groped my way to a high-backed padded chair, moaned a few times just to let my arm know that it had my sympathy. I looked around at the fantastic room. It was like nothing I had ever seen—except for a remote resemblance to Felix's underground laboratory in Tamboula. I felt an urge to laugh hysterically as I thought of the things up above, prowling the ground now, converging on the spot from which I had miraculously disappeared. How long would it be before they started to dig? The urge to laugh died.

I closed my eyes, gathered my forces, such as they were, and keened my hearing.

Rustling sounds in the earth all about me; the slow grind of the earthworm, the frantic scrabble, pause, scrabble of the burrowing mole, the soft, tentative creak of the questing root . . .

I tuned, reaching out.

Wind moaned in the trees, and their branches creaked, complaining; dry stalks rustled, clashing dead stems; soft footfalls thump-thumped, crossing the field above me. There was the growl of a turbine, coming closer, the grate of tires in soft earth. A door slammed, feet clumped.

"*It did not come this way,*" a flat voice said. Something gibbered—a sound that turned my spine to ice.

"*It is sick and weak,*" the first voice said. "*It is only a man. It did not come this way. It is not here.*"

More of the breathy gobbling; I could almost see the skull-face, the grinning mouth, the rag-tongue moving as it commanded the man-shaped slave standing before it . . .

"*It is not here,*" the humanoid said. "*I will return to my post in the village.*"

Now the gabble was angry, insistent.

"*It is not logical,*" the toneless voice said. "*It went another way. The other units will find it.*"

Other footsteps had come close. Someone walked across my grave . . .

"*There is no man here,*" another dull voice stated. "*I am going back now.*"

Two beast-things gibbered together.

"*You let it escape you at the village,*" a lifeless voice replied. "*That was not in accordance with logic.*"

The argument went on, twenty feet above my hidden sanctuary.

"*. . . a factor that we cannot compute,*" a dead voice stated. "*To remain here is unintelligent.*" Footsteps tramped away. The car door clattered open, slammed; a turbine growled into life; tires crunched the hard earth, going away.

Soft feet paced above me. Two of the creatures, possibly three, crossed and recrossed the area. I could hear them as they conferred. Then two stalked away, while the third settled down heavily to wait.

I took out my talking plastic rectangle and put it to my ear.

". . . *now in Survival Station Twelve,*" the precise voice was saying. "*Place this token in the illuminated slot on the station monitor panel.*" There was a pause. "*You are now in Survival Station Twelve . . .*"

Across the room, there was a recessed scroll-worked console dimly lit by a yellow glare strip. I wavered across to it, found the lighted slot, pressed the wafer into it, then leaned against a chair, waiting. Things clicked and hummed; a white light snapped on, giving the room a cheery, clinical look, like a Victorian parlor where a corpse was laid out. There was a preparatory buzz, matching the humming in my head; then:

"This is your Station Monitor," a deep voice said. "The voice you hear is a speech-construct, capable of verbalizing computer findings. The unit is also capable of receiving programming instruction verbally. Please speak distinctly and unambiguously. Do not employ slang or unusual constructions. Avoid words having multiple connotations . . ."

The room seemed to fade and brighten, swaying like a cable-car in a high wind. I was beginning to learn the signs; I would black out in a few seconds. I looked around for a soft place to fall, while the voice droned on. Abruptly it broke off. Then:

"Emergency override!" it said sharply. "Sensing instruments indicate you require immediate medical attention." There was a sound behind me; I turned. As if in a dream, I saw a white-sheeted cot deploy from a wall recess, roll across the room, hunting a little, then come straight on and stop beside me.

"Place yourself on the cot, with your head at the equipment end." The voice echoed from far away.

I made a vast effort, pushed myself clear of the chair, fell across the bed. I was struggling to get myself on it when I felt a touch, twisted to see padded, jointed arms grasp me and gently but firmly hoist me up and lay me out, face down. The sheet was smooth and cool under my face.

"You will undergo emergency diagnosis and treatment," the voice said. "An anesthetic will be administered if required. Do not be alarmed."

I caught just one whiff of neopolyform; then I was relaxing, letting it all go, sliding down a long, smooth slope into dark sea.

Two bosomy angels with hands like perfumed flower petals were massaging my weary limbs and crooning love songs in my ears, while not far away someone was cooking all my favorite dishes, making savory smells that put just that perfect edge on my appetite.

The cloud I was lying on was floating in sunshine, somewhere far from any conceivable discord, and I lay with my eyes closed, and blissfully enjoyed it. I deserved a rest, I realized vaguely, after all I'd gone through—whatever that was. It didn't seem important. I started to reach out to pat one of the angels, but it was really too much trouble . . .

There was a twinge from my left arm. I almost remembered something unpleasant, but it eluded me. The arm pained again, more sharply; there seemed to be only one angel now, and she was working me over in a businesslike way, ignoring my efforts to squirm free. The music had ended and the cook had quit and gone home. I must have slept right through the meal; my stomach had a hollow, unloved feeling. That angel was getting rougher all the time; maybe she wasn't an angel after all; possibly she was a real live Swedish masseuse, one of those slender, athletic blonde ones you see in the pictonews—

Ouch! Slender, hell. This one must have weighed in at a good two-fifty, and not an ounce of fat on her. What she was doing to my arm might be good for the muscle tone, but it was distinctly uncomfortable. I'd have to tell her so—just as soon as this drowsy feeling that was settling over me went away . . .

It had been a long trip, and the jogging of the oxcart was getting me down. I could feel burlap against my face; probably a bag of potatoes, from the feel of the lumps. I tried to shift to a more comfortable position, but all I could find were hard floorboards and sharp corners. I had caught my arm under one of the latter; there must have been a nail in it; it caught, and scraped, and the more I pulled away the more it hurt—

My eyes came open and I was staring at a low, gray-green ceiling perforated with tiny holes in rows, with glare strips set every few feet. There were sounds all around: busy hummings and clicks and clatters.

I twisted my head, saw a panel speckled over with more lights than a used helilot, blinking and winking and flashing in red, green, and amber . . .

I lowered my sight. I saw my arm, held out rigidly by padded metal brackets. Things like dentists' drills hovered over it, and I caught a glimpse of skin pinned back like a tent-fly, red flesh, white bone, and the glitter of clamps, set deep in a wound like the Grand Canyon.

"Your instructions are required," a deep, uninflected voice said from nowhere. "The prognosis computed on the basis of immediate amputation is 81 percent positive. Without amputation, the prognosis is 7 percent negative. Please indicate the course to be followed."

I tried to speak, got tangled up in my tongue, made another effort.

"Wha's . . . that . . . mean . . . ?"

"The organism will not survive unless the defective limb is amputated. Mutilation of a human body requires specific operator permission."

"Cu' . . . my arm . . . off . . . ?"

"Awaiting instructions."

"Die . . . 'f you don't . . . ?"

"Affirmative."

"Permission . . . granted . . ."

"Instructions acknowledged," the voice said emotionlessly. I had time to get a faint whiff of something, and then I was gone again . . .

This time, I came out of it with a sensation that took me a moment or two to analyze—a cold-water, gray-skies, no-nonsense sort of feeling. For the first time in days—how many I didn't know—the fine feverish threads of delirium were lacking in the ragged fabric of my thoughts.

I took a breath, waited for the familiar throb of pain between my temples, the first swell of the sea-sickness in my stomach. Nothing happened.

I got my eyes open and glanced over at my left arm; it was strapped to a board, swathed in bandages to the wrist, bristling with metal clips and festooned with tubing.

I felt an unaccountable surge of relief. There had been a dream—a fantastic dialogue with a cold voice that had asked . . .

In sudden panic, I moved the fingers of the hand projecting from the bandages. They twitched, flexed awkwardly. With an effort, I reached across with my right hand, touched the smooth skin of the knuckles of the other . . . Under my fingers, the texture was cool, inhumanly glossy—the cold gloss of polyon. I raked at the bandages, tore them back—

An inch above the wrist, the pseudoskin ended; a pair of gleaming metal rods replaced the familiar curve of my forearm. A sort of animal whimper came from my throat. I clenched my lost fist—and the artificial hand complied.

I fell back, feeling a numbness spread from the dead hand all through me. I was truncated, spoiled, less-than-whole. I made an effort to sit up, to tear free from the restraining straps, wild ideas of revenge boiling up inside me—

I was as weak as a drowned kitten. I lay, breathing hoarsely, getting used to the idea . . .

The Station Monitor's level voice broke into the silence:

"Emergency override now concluded. Resuming normal briefing procedure." There was a pause; then the voice went on in its tone of imperturbable calm:

"Indicate whether full status briefing is required; if other, state details of requirement."

"How long have I been unconscious?" I croaked. My voice was weak but clear.

"Question requires a value assessment of nonobjective factors; authorization requested."

"Never mind. How long have I been here?"

"Eighteen hours, twenty-two minutes, six seconds, mark. Eighteen hours, twe—"

"Close enough," I cut in. "What's been happening?"

"On the basis of the initial encephalogrammatic pattern, a preliminary diagnosis of massive anaphylactic shock coupled with acute stage-four metabolic—"

"Cancel. I don't need the gruesomer details. You've hacked off my arm, replaced it with a hook, cleared out the infection, and gotten the fever down. I guess I'm grateful. But what are the dog-things doing up above?"

There was a long silence, with just the hum of an out-of-kilter carrier. Then: "Question implies assumption at variance with previously acquired two-valued data."

"Can't you give me a simple answer?" I barked. "Have they started to dig?"

"Question implies acceptance at objective physical level of existence and activities of phenomenon classified as subjective. Closed area. Question cannot be answered."

"Wait a minute—you're telling me that the four-handed monsters and the fake humans that work with them are imaginary?"

"To avoid delays in responses, do not employ slang or unusual constructions. All data impinging on subject area both directly and indirectly, including instrument-acquired statistical material, photographic and transmitted images, audio-direct pickup, amplification, and replay, and other, have (a) been systematically rejected by Operators as incorrect, illusory, or nonobjective; (b) produced negative hallucinatory reactions resulting in inability of Operators to perceive readouts; or, (c) been followed by mental breakdown, unconsciousness, or death of Operators."

"In other words, whenever you've reported anything on the demons, the listeners either didn't believe you, couldn't see or hear your report, or went insane or died."

"Affirmative. In view of previously learned inhibition on reports of data in this sector, question cannot be answered."

"Has—ah—anything started to dig? Are there any evidences of excavation work up above?"

"Negative."

"Can the presence of this station be detected using a mass-discontinuity-type detector?"

"Negative; the station is probe-neutral."

I let out a long breath. "What is this place? Who built it? And when?"

"Station Twelve was completed in 1926. It has been periodically added to since that time. It is one of a complex of fifty survival stations prepared by the Ultimax Group."

"What's the Ultimax Group?"

"An elite inner circle organization, international in scope, privately financed, comprising one hundred and fourteen individuals selected on the basis of superior intellectual endowment, advanced specialist training, emotional stability, and other factors."

"For what purpose?"

"To monitor trends in the Basic Survival Factors, and to take such steps as may be required to maintain a favorable societal survival ratio."

"I never heard of them. How long have they been operating?"

"Two hundred and seventy-one years."

"My God! Who started it?"

"The original Committee included Benjamin Franklin, George Loffitt, Danilo Moncredi, and Cyril St. Claire."

"And Felix Severance was a member?"

"Affirmative."

"And they don't know about—the nonobjective things up above?"

"Question indeterminate, as it requires an assumption at variance with—"

"Okay—cancel. You said there are other stations. How can I get in touch with them?"

"State the number of the station with which you desire to communicate."

"What's the nearest one to Jacksonville?"

"Station Nineteen, Talisman, Florida."

"Call it."

One of the previously blank panels opposite me glowed into life, showed me a view of a room similar in many particulars to Station Twelve, except that its basic décor was a trifle more modern—the stainless steel of the early Atomic Era.

"Anybody home?" I called.

There was no reply. I tried the other stations one after another. None answered.

"That's that," I said. "Tell me more about this Ultimax Group. What's it been doing these past couple of hundred years?"

"It contributed materially to the success of the American War of Independence, the defeat of the Napoleonic Empire, the consolidation of the Italian and German nations, the emergence of Nippon, the defeat of the Central Powers in the First Engagement of the European War, and of the Axis Powers in the Second Engagement, and the establishment of the State of Israel. It supported the space effort . . ."

I was beginning to feel a little ragged now; the first fine glow was fading. I listened to the voice for another half-hour, while it told me all about the little-known facts of history; then I dismissed it and took another nap.

I ate, slept, and waited. After fourteen hours, the straps holding my arm down released themselves; after that, I practiced tottering up and down my prison, testing my new arm, and now and then tuning in on what went on overhead. For the most part, there was silence, broken only by the sounds of nature and the slap and thump of pacing feet. I heard a few gobbled conversations, and once an exchange between a humanoid and a demon:

"It has means of escaping pursuit," the flat voice was saying as I picked it up. *"This is the same one that eluded our units at location totter-pohl."*

Angry sounds from a demon.

"That is not my area of surveillance," the first voice said coldly. *"My work is among the men."*

Another alien tongue-lashing.

"All reports are negative; the instruments indicate nothing—"

An excited interruption.

"When the star has set, then. I must call in more units . . ." The voice faded, going away.

"Monitor, it's time for me to start making plans. They're getting restless up above. I'm going to need a few things: clothes, money, weapons, transportation. Can you help me?"

"State your requirements in detail."

"I need an inconspicuous civilian-type suit, preferably heated. I'll also need underwear, boots, and a good hand-gun; one of those Borgia Specials Felix gave me would do nicely. About ten thousand cees in cash—some small bills, the rest in hundreds. I want a useful ID—and a good map. I don't suppose you could get me an OE suit and a lift-belt, but a radar-negative car would be very useful—a high-speed, armored job."

"The garments will be ready momentarily. The funds must be facsimile-reproduced from a sample. Those on hand are of last year's issue and thus invalid. The Borgia Special is unknown; further data required. You will be given directions to the nearest Ultimax garage, where you may make a selection of helis and ground effect cars."

I got out my wallet, now nearly flat; I picked out five and ten cee notes and a lone hundred.

"Here are your patterns; I hope you can vary the serial numbers."

"Affirmative. Please supply data on Borgia Special."

"That's a 2mm needler, with a special venom. It's effective on these nonexistent phenomena up above."

"A Browning 2mm will be supplied; the darts will be charged with UG formula nine twenty-three toxin. Please place currency samples in slot G on the main console."

I followed instructions. Within half an hour the delivery bin had disgorged a complete wardrobe, including a warm, sturdy, and conservatively-cut suit with a special underarm pocket in which the needler nestled snugly; my wallet bulged with nicely aged bills. I had a late-model compass-map strapped to my wrist, a card identifying me as a Treasury man, and a special key tucked in an inner pocket that would open the door to a concealed Ultimax motor depot near Independence, less than thirty miles away. I was equipped to leave now—as soon as I was strong enough.

More hours passed. At regular intervals, the Station Monitor gave instructions for treatment, keeping tabs on my condition by means of an array of remote-sensing instruments buried in the walls. My strength was returning slowly; I had lost a lot of weight, but the diet of nourishing concentrates the station supplied was replacing some of that, too.

The arm was a marvel of bioprosthetics. The sight of the stark, functional chromalloy radius and ulna still gave me a strange, unpleasant sensation every time I saw it, but I was learning to use it; as the nerve-connections healed, I was even developing tactile sensitivity in the fingertips.

When the chronometer on the wall showed that I had been in the underground station for forty-nine hours, I made another routine inquiry about conditions up above.

"How about it, Monitor?" I called. "Any signs of excavation work going on up there?"

There was a long pause—as there was every time I asked questions around the edges of the Forbidden Topic.

"Negative," the voice said at last.

"They've had time enough now to discover I'm not hiding under the rug in some nearby motel. I wonder what they're waiting for?"

There was no answer. But then I hadn't really asked a question.

"Make another try to raise one of the other stations," I ordered. I watched the screen as one equipment-crowded room after another flashed into view. None answered my call.

"What about those other Station Monitors?" I asked. "Can I talk to them?"

"Station Monitors are aspects of the Central Co-ordinating Monitor," the voice said casually. "All inquiries may be addressed directly to any local station unit."

"You don't volunteer much, do you?" I inquired rhetorically.

"Negative," the voice replied solemnly.

"Can you get a message out to somebody for me?"

"Affirmative, assuming—"

"Skip the assumptions. He's somewhere in Jacksonville, Florida—if the demons didn't kill him just to keep in practice—and if he followed my instructions to stay in town. His name's Joel—last name unknown, even to him. Address unknown. As of a week ago, he was crewman aboard a sub-tanker called the *Excalibur*, out of New Hartford. Find him, and tell him to meet me at the main branch of the YMNA in ... where's the nearest diplomatic post?"

"The British Consulate at Chicago."

"All right. I want Joel to meet me in the lobby of the main Y in Chicago, as soon as he can get there. Do you think you can reach him with what I've given you?"

"Indeterminate. Telephone connections can be made with—"

There was a loud, dull-toned *thump!* that shook the station. The Monitor's voice wavered and went on: "—all points on—" Another thud.

I was on my feet, watching microscopic dust particles shaken out of crevices by the impact, settling to the floor. There was another blow, more severe than the others. "What the hell was that?" I asked—yelled—but it was rhetorical.

The demons were at my door.

"All right, talk fast, Monitor," I barked. I pulled on my new clothes, checked the gun as I talked. "Is there any other route out of here?"

"The secondary exit route leads from the point now indicated by the amber light," the voice said imperturbably. Across the room, I saw an indicator blink on, off, on. "However," the Monitor went on, "departure from the Station at this time is not advised. You have not yet recovered full normal function. Optimum recovery rate will be obtained by continued bed rest, controlled diet, proper medication, and minimal exertion—"

"You're developing a nagging tone," I told it. "Get that door open. Where does it lead?"

"The tunnel extends seventeen hundred yards on a bearing of two-one-nine debouching within a structure formerly employed for the storage of ensilage."

"Good old Ultimax; they don't miss a bet." Another blow racked the station.

I buttoned up my pin-stripe weather suit, adjusted the thermostat, settled the gun under my arm.

"Monitor, I'm feeling pretty good, but you'd better give me an extra shot of vitamins to get me through the next few hours. It's a long walk to that garage."

"The use of massive stimulants at this time—"

"That's the idea: massive stimulants—" There was another heavy blow against the station walls. "Hurry up; your counseling will have to wait for a more leisurely phase in my career. How about that shot?"

With much verbal clucking, the cybernetic circuits complied. I held my good arm in the place indicated, and took an old-fashioned needle injection that the Monitor assured me would keep me ticking over like a le Mans speedster for at least forty-eight hours. It started to tell me what would happen then, but I cut it off.

"I'm tougher than you think. Now, how can I contact you—or the Central Monitor—from outside?"

The level voice gave me a long triple code. "Dial on any public communication screen," it added. "The circuits will respond to patterns inherent in your vocalization characteristics. This service is to be employed only in the event of severe emergency involving a major Ultimax program."

I took a moment to run through a simple mnemonic exercise. Then:

"Monitor, I assume you're mined for destruction?"

"Affirmative."

"Wait until the last minute—until there's a nice crowd of curious zombies and other nonexistent phenomena around; then blow. Understand?"

"Affirmative," the voice said calmly.

I went to the narrow exit panel, paused. "Monitor, how do you feel about blasting yourself out of existence? I mean do you care?"

"Question requires value-judgment outside the scope of installed circuitry," the voice said.

"Yours not to reason why, eh? I guess you're lucky at that. It's not dying that hurts—it's living." I took a last look back at the station. It wasn't homey, but it had saved my life.

"So long," I called.

There was no answer. I stepped through into the narrow corridor.

I reached the ascending staircase at the end of the mile-long, tile-walled tunnel. I fumbled, found an electro-latch of unfamiliar design. With a whining of gears, a heavy trap door lifted. I emerged into icy-cold, dusty-smelling darkness, felt my way across to a collapsing metal door. As I pushed it aside, the metal crumpled under my hand like tinfoil. I still felt weak, but I had my old grip back.

Out on the pot-holed blacktop drive under a black sky, an arctic wind slashed at me. After the days underground, the fresh air smelled good. I turned up my thermostat and started off across the open field to the north.

I had gone perhaps a hundred yards, when a sudden glare erupted into the sky from over the brow of the low ridge to my right, followed almost instantly by a tremor underfoot. A mile away, a column of red-lit smoke boiled upward.

Nearer at hand, there was a rumble from the ancient silo; I turned in time to see the door leap from its fastenings and whirl away, driven by the concussion that had traveled along the tunnel. A cloud of dust rolled across toward me. Then I heard the belated sound of the blast; a deep *carrumph!* that rolled across like thunder from the site of Survival Station Twelve. I threw myself flat, hearing bits of debris from the silo thump around me.

Other debris was raining around me now—new arrivals from the main blast. Clods thumped off my back. Something heavier fell with a bone-cracking thump, bounced high over me, struck again, and rolled.

All was silent now; the ruddy cloud rose higher, fading; I got to my feet and went over to the heavy object that had fallen. It was a major fragment of the body of one of the dog-things.

Chapter Eleven

I walked for seven hours, following the tiny illuminated chart projected on the thumbnail-sized screen
of the compass-map, and thinking of a hundred
questions I could have asked the all-wise moron
that called itself the Station Monitor, if I had had
just a few minutes more. Probably, as soon as the
demons' cordon had revealed that I hadn't escaped
the area, they had started poking around at random in the ever-narrowing circle. It had taken their
probes this long to hit upon the buried station. I
could take a small measure of comfort from the
fact that they hadn't found it sooner.

Near dawn, I reached a scattering of tumble-
down farm buildings from which the glow of the
town was visible a mile or two to the north. Following instructions, I made my way past ranked
wheat elevators, took an abandoned wheel-road
that angled off to the northwest, and came to the
row of tractor sheds that the Monitor had told me
housed the Ultimax Transport depot.

I tried doors, finally got one open, did more groping in dusty darkness, and found the hidden switch that rolled back a section of rubbish-littered floor to reveal a heavy car-lift.

I rode it down into a wide storage garage, where eight ground cars and four helis were parked, bright with polished enamel and chromalloy. Two of the cars were ancient internal-combustion jobs, of interest only to museums. The depot, it seemed, had been in operation for some time. Another vehicle, an oversized heli, had an occupant—a desiccated corpse, dressed in the style of twenty years before. The maintenance machines were programmed to remove dirt and dents, refuel and service the vehicles—but a malfunctioning operator was beyond them.

I picked a late-model heli with armorplast all around, and an inconspicuous battery of small-bore infinite repeaters mounted under the forward cooling grid. I tried the turbines; they whirred into life after half a minute's cranking. I trundled the machine to the elevator, rode up, closed the garage behind me, and lifted off into the night sky.

Just after sunrise a small all-day-for-a-cee parking raft anchored two miles off Chicago accepted my heli with a reassuring sneer of indifference. I took the ski-way ashore, hailed a cab, and flitted across the vast sprawl of the city to drop into a tiny heli-park nestled like a concrete glade in the mighty forest of masonry all around.

I paid off the driver, and rode a walkway half a mile to the block-square cube of unwashed glass that housed the central offices and famous five-thousand-bed dormitory of the Young Men's Non-denominational Association.

I left word for Joel, asked for and received one of the six-by-eight private cubicles. I dropped a half-cee in the slot for a breakfast-table edition pic-tonews, and settled down to wait.

Hours slipped by while I slept—a restless sleep, from which I awoke with a start, again and again, hearing the creak of the floor, the rattle of a latch along the corridor. I wasn't hungry; the thought of food made my stomach knot. There was a taste in my mouth like old gym shoes, and a full set of nausea-and-headache symptoms hovered in the wings, ready to come on at the first hint of encouragement.

I shaved once, staring at a grim, hollow-cheeked face in the mirror. The plastic-surgery scars were pale lines now, but the shortened nose, lowered hairline, blue eyes, and pale crewcut still looked as unnatural to me as a Halloween false-face.

I tried to estimate how long it might be before Joel arrived—if he arrived. It had been five hours since I had given the order to the Monitor. A message would have gone out to Station Nine; the Monitor there would have connections with a telefax or visiscreen switchboard. The order would have gone to a legman—perhaps an ordinary messenger service, or a private detective agency. Someone would have followed the slim leads, checked out the habitual places where Joel spent his time between voyages. It was safe to assume that he was a creature of habit. Once the message—with funds, I hoped—was delivered, Joel would be steered to a tube or jet station. Allow two hours for the passage, another hour for him to discover the cross-town kwik-stop . . .

The arithmetic always gave the same answer: he should have been here an hour or two after I arrived.

I called the desk again. Nothing. It had been nine hours now; if he didn't show in another hour, I would have to go on without him. I thought of trying a special code call to the Ultimax Central

Monitor, but I couldn't quite classify the situation as a severe emergency—not yet.

The tenth hour came and went. I got off the bed, groaning; aches were beginning to creep through the armor of drugs. It was time to move, Joel or no Joel. I had a plan—not much of one, but the best I could do alone.

I dressed, went down to the vast, echoing lobby. It was as cheery as a gas chamber. A few hundred derelicts lounged in rump-sprung chairs parked on patches of dusty rug, islands in a sea of plastic flooring the color of dried mud. I crossed to the information desk, opened my mouth—and saw Joel stretched out in a chair like a battered boxer between rounds, eyes shut, mouth open, an electric-blue scarf knotted around his thick neck like a hangman's noose.

I felt my face cracking into a wide grin. I went over to him, shook him gently, then a little harder. His eyes opened. He looked at me blankly for a moment—his eyes like the windows of an empty house. Then he smiled.

"Hi, Jones," he said, sitting up. "Boy, you should've seen the train I rode in! It was all fancy, and there was this nice lady . . ." He told me all about it while we gripped hands, grinning. Suddenly, now, it was all right. Luck was still with me. The demons had tried—tried hard—but I was here, still alive, iron hands and all—and I wasn't alone. I felt a hint of spring return to my muscles, the first twinge of hunger in days.

The British Consulate, perched on piles on the shore of Lake Michigan, was a weather-stained cube of stone filigree done in the sterilized Hindu style popular in the nineties. There were lights beyond the grillwork in the wide entry, and on the upper floors.

We walked past once, then turned, came back,

went up the wide, shallow steps, past a steaming fountain of recirculated, heated water glimmering in a purple spotlight. I rattled the tall grille. A Royal Marine three-striper in traditional dress blues got up from a desk, came across the wide marble floor to the gate, fingering the hilt of a ceremonial saber.

"The Consulate opens at ten I.M.," he said, looking me over through the grille.

"My name's Jones," I said. "Treasury. I've got to see the Duty Officer—now. It can't wait until morning."

"Let's see a little identification, sir," the marine said.

I showed him the blue class one I.D. He nodded, handed the card back through the grille. He opened up, stood back, and watched Joel follow me inside.

"Where does the Duty Officer stay?" I asked.

"That's Mr. Phipps tonight. He's got a room upstairs. He's up there now." The expression on the sergeant's face suggested that this was a mixed blessing. "I'll ring him," he added. "You'll 'ave to wite 'ere."

I stood where I could see the approach to the building while the sergeant went to a desk, dialed, talked briefly. A second marine came along the corridor and took up a position opposite me. He was a solidly built redhead, not over eighteen. He looked at me with a face as expressionless as a courthouse clock.

" 'E's coming down," the sergeant said. He looked across at the other marine. "What do you want, Dyvis?"

The redhead kept his eyes on me. "Breff o' fresh air," he said shortly.

There was a sound of feet coming leisurely down the winding staircase on my left. A sad-looking tweed-suited man with thinning gray hair and pale blue eyes in wrinkled pockets came into view. He slowed when he saw me, glanced at the two marines.

"What's this all about, Sergeant?" he said in a tired voice, like someone who has put up with a lot lately.

"Somebody to see you," the sergeant said. "Sir," he added. The newcomer looked at me suspiciously.

"I have some important information, Mr. Phipps," I said.

"Just who are you, might I inquire?" Phipps asked. His expression indicated that whatever I said, he wouldn't be pleased.

"U.S. Treasury." I showed him the I.D.

He nodded and looked past me, out through the heavy grille-work. He waved toward the stair.

"You may as well come along to the office." He turned and started back up; I followed him to the second floor, along a wide, still corridor of dark offices. We entered a lighted room with sexless furnishing in the international official medium-plush style.

Phipps sat down behind a cluttered desk, looked across at me glumly as I took a chair. Joel stood beside me, gaping at the picture of Queen Anne on the wall.

"I won't bore you with details, Mr. Phipps," I said. "I've seen some pretty odd goings-on lately." I looked bashful. "It sounds funny, I know, but . . . well, it involves a kind of unusual dog . . ."

I watched his expression closely. He was eyeing me with a bored expression that suggested this was about what he'd expect from cranks who rattled the grille at an hour when civilized people were sipping the third drink of the evening in an embassy drawing-room somewhere.

He patted back a yawn.

"Just how are British interests involved, Mr.—ah—Jones?"

"Well, this dog was intelligent," I said.

"Well!" His eyebrows went up. "I'm sure I don't—"

Footsteps were coming along the hall. I turned. A husky, black-haired man with deep-set dark eyes came into the room, looked at me, ignoring Phipps. I saw the redheaded marine in the hall behind him. I felt my pulse start to beat a little faster.

"What is it you want here?" he snapped.

"Ah, Mr. Clomesby-House, Mr. Jones, of the American Treasury Department," Phipps said, adjusting a look of alert interest on his dried-out features. I surmised that Clomesby-House was his boss.

"Mr. Jones was just lodging a complaint regarding a—um—dog," Phipps said.

Clomesby-House narrowed his eyes at me. "What dog is this?"

"I realize it sounds a little strange," I said, smiling diffidently, "but—well, let me start at the beginning."

"Just one moment." The black-eyed man held up a hand. "Perhaps we'd better discuss this matter in private." He stepped back, waved a hand toward the door. Phipps looked surprised.

"Certainly," I said. "It sounds crazy, but—"

I followed Clomesby-House along a corridor, with Joel beside me and the marine trailing. At the door to a roomy office, I paused, eyeing the marine.

"Ah—this is pretty confidential," I said behind my hand. "Perhaps the guard should wait outside?"

Clomesby-House shot me a black look, opened his mouth to object.

"Unless you're afraid I might be dangerous, or something," I added, showing him a smirk.

He snorted. "That's all, Davis. Return to your post."

I closed the door carefully, went across and took a chair by the desk behind which the black-eyed man had seated himself. Joel sat on my left.

"Tell me just what it is you've seen," Clomesby-House said, leaning forward.

"Well." I laughed shyly. "It sounds pretty silly, here in a nice clean office—but some funny things have been happening to me lately. They all seem to center around the dogs . . ."

He waited.

"It's a secret spy network—I'm sure of it," I went on. "I have plenty of evidence. Now, I don't want you just to take my word for it. I have a friend who's been helping me—"

His dark eyes went to Joel. "This man knows of this, too?"

"Oh, he's not the one I meant. He just gave me a lift over. I've told him a little." I chuckled again. "But he says it's all in my head. I had a little accident some months ago—have a metal plate in my skull, as a matter of fact—But never mind that. My friend and I know better. These dogs—"

"You have seen them—often?"

"Well, every now and then."

"And why did you come here—to the British Consulate?" he shot at me.

"I'm coming to that part. You see—well, actually, it's a little hard to explain. If I could just show you . . ."

I looked anxious—like a nut who wants to reveal the location of a flying saucer, but is a little shy about butterfly nets. "If you could possibly spare the time—I'd like you to meet my friend. It's not far."

He was still squinting at me. His fingers squeaked as he tensed them against the desk-top. I remembered Julius exhibiting the same mannerism—a nervous habit of the not-men when they had a decision to make. I could almost hear him thinking; it would be simplicity itself for him to summon the strait-jacket crew, let them listen to my remarks about intelligent dogs, and let nature take its course. But on the other hand, what I had to say just might alert someone, cause unwelcome inquiries, invite troublesome poking about . . .

He came to a decision. He stood, smiling a plaster smile.

"Perhaps that would be best," he said. "There is only one person beside yourselves—" he glanced at Joel—"who knows of this?"

"That's right; it's not the kind of thing a fellow spreads around." I got to my feet. "I hope it's not too much trouble," I said, trying to look a little embarrassed now. Flying-saucer viewers aren't accustomed to willing audiences.

"I said I would accompany you," Clomesby-House snapped. "We will go now—immediately."

"Sure—swell," I said. I scrambled to the door and held it for him. "I have my car—"

"That will not be necessary. We will take an official vehicle."

I showed him a sudden suspicious look. After all, I didn't want just anybody to see my saucer. "But no driver," I specified. "Just you and me and Joel here."

He gave a Prussian nod. "As you wish. Come along."

He led the way to the Consulate garage on the roof, dismissed the marine on duty, and took the controls of a fast, four-seater despatch heli. I got in beside him, and Joel sat in the rear.

I gave directions for an uninhabited area to the northwest—Yerkes National Forest—and we lifted off, hurtled out across the sprawl of city lights and into darkness.

Forty-five minutes later, with my nose against the glass, I stared down at a vast expanse of unbroken blackness spread out below.

"This is the place," I said. "Set her down right here."

Clomesby-House shot me a look that would have curdled spring water. "Here?" he growled.

I nodded brightly. It was as good a place as any for what I had in mind. He hissed, angled the heli sharply downward. I could sense that he was beginning to regret his excessive caution in whisking me away to a lonely place where he could deal with me and my imaginary accomplice privately. He had wasted time and fuel on an idiot who was no more than a normal mental case after all. I could almost hear him deciding to land, kill me and Joel with a couple of chops of his jack-hammer hands, and hurry back to whatever zombies did in their leisure hours. The thought of caution didn't so much as cross his mind. After all, what were we but a pair of soft, feeble humans?

I thought of the arm he and his friends had cost me, and felt both fists—the live and the dead—clenching in anticipation.

Clomesby-House was either an excellent pilot or a fool. He whipped the heli in under the spreading branches of a stand of hundred-foot hybrid spruce, grounded it without a jar. He slammed a door open, letting in a wintry blast, and climbed out. The landing lights burned blue-white pools on the patchy snow, flickering as the rotor blades spun to a stop.

"Stay behind me, Joel," I said quickly. "No matter what happens, don't interfere. Just keep alert for the dog-things; you understand?"

He gave me a startled look. "Are they gonna come here, Jones?"

"I hope not." I jumped out, stood facing Clomesby House. Behind me, Joel hugged himself, staring around at the great trees.

"Very well," the not-man said, his black eyes probing me like cold pokers. "Where is the other man?" He stood in a curious slack position, like a mannikin that hasn't been positioned by the window dresser. Out here, with just two soon-to-be-dead humans watching, it wasn't necessary to bother with all the troublesome details of looking human.

I went close to him, stared into his face.

"Never mind all that," I said. "It was just a come-on. It's you I want to talk to. Where did you come from? What do you want on Earth?"

All the expression went out of his face. He stood for a moment, as though considering a suggestion.

I knew the signs; he was communing with another inhuman brain, somewhere not too distant. I stepped up quickly, hit him in the pit of the stomach with all my strength.

He bounced back like a tackle dummy hit by a swinging boom, crashed against a tree-trunk, rebounded—still on his feet. In the instant of contact, I had felt something break inside him—but it wasn't slowing him down. He launched himself at me, hands outstretched. I met him with a straight right smash to the head that spun him, knocked him to the ground. He scrabbled, sending great gouts of frozen mud and snow flying. He came to his feet, lunged at me, reaching—

I leaned aside from a grasping hand, chopped him below the point of the shoulder, felt bone snap. He staggered, and I took aim, struck at his head—

I hadn't even seen the tree that fell on me. I groped my way to my feet, feeling the blood running across my jaw, blinking my vision clear . . .

The thing shaped like a man came toward me, expressionless, one arm hanging, the other raised, hand flattened for an axblow. I raised my steel arm, took an impact like a trip-hammer, countered with a smashing chestpunch. It was a waste of effort; the thing's thoracic area was armored like a dinosaur's skull. It brought its arm around in a swipe that caught me glancingly across the shoulder, sent me reeling.

Joel was between us, huge fists ready; he landed a smashing left that would have felled an ox, followed with a right that struck the cold, smooth face like a cannonball. The creature seemed not to notice. It struck out, and Joel staggered, caught himself—and a second blow sent him skidding. Then the thing was past him, charging for me. Joel's diversion had given me the time to set myself. I caught the descending arm in a two-handed grip, hauled it around, broke it across my chest. I hurled the alien from me. Then, as it tripped and fell, I aimed a kick that caught it on the kneecap. It went down, and I stood over it breathing hard, as it threshed helplessly, silently, trying to rise on its broken leg.

"Don't struggle," I got out between breaths. "That wouldn't be logical, would it? Now it's time for you to tell me a few things. Where did you come from? What world?"

It lay still then, a broken toy, no longer needed. "You will die soon," it said flatly.

"Maybe; meanwhile just call me curious. Where's your headquarters? Who runs things, you or the dogs? What do you do with the men you steal—or their brains?"

"Information is of no use to the soon-dead," the flat voice stated indifferently.

Behind me, Joel moaned—a thin, high wail of animal torment. I whirled to him. He lay oddly crumpled at the base of a giant tree, his face white, shocked. Blood ran from his mouth. I went to him, knelt, and tried to ease him to a more comfortable position.

Another cry came from his open mouth—a mindless cry of pure agony. I laid him out on his back, opened his jacket.

The front of his shirt was a sodden mass of bloody fabric. The thing's blow had smashed his chest as effectively as a falling safe.

"Joel, hold on—I'll get you to a doctor." I eased my arms under him, started to lift.

He shrieked, twisted once—then went limp.

My hand went to his wrist, found a pulse, weak, unsteady—but he was alive. His eyelids fluttered, opened.

"I fell down," he said clearly.

"I'll get you into the heli." My voice was choked.

"It hurt my head," Joel went on. "But now it don't hurt ..." His mouth twitched. His tongue touched his lips. The shadow of a frown came over his face.

"It tickles in my head," he said. "I don't like it when it tickles in my head. I don't want the dogs to come, Jones. I'm afraid."

"The dogs?" I felt my scalp tighten. I twisted, staring into the forest, saw nothing. "Come on, Joel; I'm going to lift you into the heli." I put a hand under his back, half-lifted him. He screamed hoarsely. I lowered him again.

"It hurts too bad, Jones," he gasped out. "I'm sorry."

"Where are the dogs, Joel?"

"They're close." His eyes sought me. His tongue licked his lips again. "I know—you got to go now, Jones. I'm sorry I yelled and all."

I whirled on the broken man-thing. "How far away are they?" I snapped. "You called them; how long before they'll be here?"

It looked at me with the one eye that remained in its battered head, and said nothing. I kicked it in the side, sent the limp body skidding two yards.

"Talk, damn you!"

It merely looked at me, as impersonally as a morgue attendant taking inventory. Its gaze went past me; it seemed to be listening ...

Then I felt it—the greasy, gray feeling of unreality that meant the demons were closing in. I keened my hearing ...

I heard the lope of demonic hands galloping across frozen ground, brushing against brittle, leafless twigs, coming closer.

"You . . . gotta . . . hurry . . . up . . ." Joel's voice croaked. "G'bye, Jones. You was . . . a good friend. I guess . . . you was . . . the only friend . . . I ever had . . ."

He was dying; I knew nothing I could do would save him. And a few feet away the heli waited, fueled and ready. I wanted to go.

But I couldn't do it.

"Take it easy, Joel," I said hoarsely. "I'm not leaving. I'm staying with you."

He opened his mouth, but no sound came out.

There was a crash of underbrush. As I whirled, a dark dog-shape bounded from the shadow of a giant tree, turned, and charged into the circle of light. I set myself. As it leaped, I threw my weight into a straight-arm blow that met the bony face in midair, drove it back in pulped ruin into the shattered skull. The thing hurtled past me, struck, threshing in its death-fit.

Two more of the beast-things leaped into view, sprang at me side by side. I caught one by the neck, crushed bone and hide together, hurled it aside. I turned to drive a kick into the chest of the second as it rounded on me. I jumped after it, smashed its head with a left and right as it rose up, snapping.

There were more of them around me now. I spun, kicked at one, struck another down with my chromalloy fist, shook a third from my right arm, fended off another . . . It was a nightmare battle against leaping creatures almost impalpable to my PAPA-reinforced blows; they came at me like bounding ghost-shapes, red-eyed and gape-jawed. I struck, and struck, and struck again . . .

A white-hot bear-trap closed on my leg. I tried to shake it off. It clung, dragging at me. Jaws snapped

an inch from my throat. I hammered at a skull-
face, saw it crumble—and another sprang up. One
struck me from beyind. I stumbled, felt jaws like a
saw-edged vise clamp on my thigh. There was one
at my left arm now; I heard its teeth break against
the steel rods. With my free hand, I struck at it;
then two of the things leaped at once, fastened on
my good arm—

I twisted away from jaws that lunged for my
throat, felt myself falling. Then I was down, and
the weight on me was like heaped mattresses set
with needles of fire; I was like a man drowning in
a sea of piranha—razor teeth stripping the flesh
from the living bone . . .

I was on my back, a cluster of demon faces over
me like surgeons over an operating table; teeth
snapped, ripped at my throat; I felt the tearing of
flesh, the gush of scalding blood. As if in a dream,
I heard the gabble of demon voices, the slap of
beast hands. Then blackness closed over me. I knew
it was death.

Chapter Twelve

Somewhere, I dream in a sunless emptiness where the years arch like ancient elms over the long avenue of time—a path across eternity, without a beginning and without end.

Into the static universe, change comes: a sense of subtle pressures, of energy-fields in transition. An imbalance grows—and with the imbalance a need—and from the need, volition. I sense movement, the slide and turn of intricate components, and the tentative questing of sensors, like raw nerves hesitantly exposed. Light, form, color impinge on delicate instruments. Space takes on dimension, texture.

All around me, a broad plain of shattered rock and black shadows stretches away to a line of fire at the edge of the world, under the glare of a sun that rages purple-white against bottomless silver-black.

A shape moves, small with distance—beyond it, others. I am moving too, driving forward effortlessly over the rough ground, throwing up dust in heavy clouds that drop back with a curious quickness. Rock-

chips fly, twinkling as they fall. I sense vibrations; the thunder of my passage, the whine and growl of meshing metal, the oscillation of electrons.

Abruptly, from beyond the jagged horizon, an object comes, a glittering torpedo-shape tipped with blue fire, flashing with a swiftness that swells it in a movement to giant size. I feel the closing of relays within me; circuits come alive. My back arches; I lift my arms and thrust—

Fire lances from my fingertips, a silent stuttering of brilliance across the sky. I pivot, trailing the shattered projectile as it gouts incandescence, breaks apart, falls in fragments beyond a distant stony ridge. A growl of thunder rolls, dies. I rake my eyes across the desolate spread of fragmented shale around me, mark a flicker of movement among up-tilted rock-slabs, point and fire in one smooth, coordinated motion . . .

And still I plunge on, charging to a blind attack against an unknown enemy.

I grind down a long slope, dozing aside rock-chunks, jolting across crevases. A vast shape swings from an inky shadow to my left, pivots heavily, trailing a shattered tread—dreadnaught of the enemy, damaged, left behind in the retreat, but with its offensive power intact. I see the immense disrupter grid swing to bear on me, glow to red heat—

I lock full emergency power to my prime batteries, open my mouth, and bellow—and bellow again . . .

Then I am racing off-side, driving for the crest of a ridge, over, down the far slope as molten rock bubbles behind me. The shock wave strikes and I am lifted, flung down-slope. I catch myself, claw for purchase; the limping monster appears on the ridge and I hurl my thunder at it and see its exposed grid shatter, explode . . .

I turn back to rejoin my column, aware of the drive of mighty gears and shafts, of curving plates of flintsteel and chromalloy, of the maze of neurotronic *linkages that run to command-ganglia, and from these secondary centers to the thousand sensors, controls, mechanisms, reflex circuits that are my nervous system. Far away, I feel a momentary stir of remote phantom memories—faint echoes of a forgotten dream of life ... but the recollection fades, is forgotten.*

I swing up across a slanting rock-shelf, take up my position on the flank of a fire-spouting behemoth bearing the symbol of a Centurion. The battle continues ...

I fight, responding automatically to each emergency with the instant reaction of drilled reflexes—but in among the incisive commands of my response circuits, meaningless wisps of thought flash like darting fishes:

Wheel left into line, advance in file ... dry-looking country; a long way between bars ... *Main battery, arm; primary quadrant, saturation fire* ... What is this place? A hell of a strange sky ... *Defensive armor, category nine; blank visual sensors for flash at minus twelve microseconds, mark* ... Air-bursts all around, looks like a battle going on; what am I doing here? *Advance at assault speed; arm secondary batteries, omega shields in position* ... The dust—it's thick as Georgia clay—but I secm to see through it, beyond it—

"UNIT EIGHTY-FOUR! DAMAGE REPORT!"

The words flash into my mind like the silent blow of a bright ax, not spoken in English, but spat in an abbreviated Command code of harsh inflected syllables. I hear myself acknowledge the order in kind, as in instant compulsive response my damage sensors race through a fifty-thousand-item checklist like rats scurrying among filled shelves. "Negative," *I hear myself report.* "All systems functional."

But deep inside me a dam strains, cracks, bursts. A tendril of released thought, startled awake by the command, seems to grope, struggling outward. Word-images, sharp-chiseled as diamonds, thrust among the bodiless conceptualizations of rote conditioning. I reach back, back—to the blinding light of a strange awakening, past confusion and dawning awareness . . . back . . . into a bland, ever-dwindling record of stimulus, pain, stimulus, pleasure; a wordless voice that speaks, instructs, impresses, punishes, rewards—printing on my receptive mind the skein of conditioned reflex, the teachings that convert the blanked protoplasm of the shocked brain into the trained battle-computer of a dreadnaught of the line . . .

And in the forefront of my mind, I am remembering: somewhere long ago, a body—of flesh and blood, soft, complex, infinitely responsive—

A target flashes, and I aim and fire—

That impulse had once lifted an arm, pointed a finger. A human finger; a human body! I savor the concept, at once strange and as familiar as life itself. The fragile concept of identity crystallized from vagueness, grows, sharpens—

There is a moment of disorientation, a swirling together and a rending apart.

I am a man. A man named Bravais.

"UNIT EIGHTY-FOUR! RECHECK NAVIGATIONAL GRID FOR GROSS POSITIONAL ERROR!" The habit of obedience carried me forward over rough ground, maneuvering in response to long-learned rules as rigid as laws of nature. My sensors lanced out, locked to my fellow machines; my control mechanisms acted, swinging me to the point of zero-stress, then driving me forward—and in my mind, thoughts jostled each other:

Secondary target, track! . . . *If you meet another Julius, break him in two and keep going* . . . advance, assault speed . . . *This is your Station Monitor; permission requested to mutilate the body* . . .

Arm all batteries; ten-microsecond alert . . . *I guess you was the only friend I ever had—*

Suddenly, vividly I remembered the fight with the demons, the weight of the stinking bodies that bore me down, teeth tearing at my throat . . .

I had seen the enemy at work—the deft saws, the clever scalpels.

I remembered the brain of the Algerian major, lifted from the skull, preserved—

As mine was now preserved.

The demons had killed my body, left it to rot in the forest. But now I lived again—in the body of a great machine.

"UNIT EIGHTY-FOUR: REPORT!"

The command struck at me—a mental impulse of immense power. I watched, an observer aloof from the action, as my conditioned-response complex reacted, sensing the fantastic complexity of the workings of the mobile fort that was now my body.

"RETIRE TO POSITION IN SECONDARY TIER!" The harsh order galvanized my automatic responses in instant obedience—

On impulse, I intercepted the command; then I reached out along my circuits, sent out new commands. I turned myself, faced the violent sun, moved ponderously forward; I halted, pivoted, tracked my guns across the dark sky. Somehow, I had gained control of my machine-body. I remembered the command—the external voice that would have asserted its control—

But instead, it had cued my hypnotically-produced reserve personality-fraction into active control.

I withdrew, felt the automatics resume control, moving me off to my new station. The aliens were clever, and as thorough as death; I had been tracked down, killed, chained in slavery on a ruined no-man's world; but I had broken the bonds. I was alive, master of my fortress-body—free, inside the enemy defenses!

Later—hours or days, I had no way of knowing—I rumbled down an echoing tunnel into a vast cavern, took my place in a long line of scarred battle units.

"UNIT EIGHTY-FOUR: FALL OUT!" the command voice bellowed soundlessly. I moved forward. Other units moved up, stationed themselves on either side of me. A long silence grew. I was aware that other orders were being given—orders not addressed to me, automatically tuned out by my trained reflexes. Something was going on . . .

I made an effort, extended sensitivity, picked up the transmission:

"—malfunction! Escort Unit Eight-four to interrogation chamber and stand by during reflex-check! Acknowledge and execute!"

I heard the snick of relays closing; I was hearing the internal command circuits of my fellow battle units.

"UNIT EIGHTY-FOUR: PROCEED TO INTERROGATION CHAMBER!"

I let my automaton-circuits stir me into motion. I moved off, listening as the command voice gave a final instruction to my armed guard:

"Units Eighty-three and Eighty-five: at first indication of deviant response, trigger destruct circuits!"

I saw the turrets of the battle wagons beside me swing to cover me; their ports slid back, the black snouts of infinite repeaters emerged, aimed and ready. The command-mind had already sensed something out of the ordinary in Unit Eighty-four.

I rolled on toward the interrogation chamber, monitoring the flow of reflex-thought in the minds of the units beside me—a dull sequence of course-correction, alert-reinforcements, routine functional adjustments. Carefully, using minimal power, I reached out . . .

"Unit Eighty-three; damage report!" I commanded.

Nothing happened. The battle units were programmed to accept commands from only one source—the Command voice.

"Units Eight-three and Eighty-five: arm weapons; complete prefire drill!" The command came. From beside me, I heard arming locks slide open. Together, my guards and I entered the armored test cell.

"UNIT EIGHTY-FOUR! DISARM AND LOCK ALL WEAPONS! RESPONSE-SEQUENCE ALPHA, EXECUTE!" The voice of the Interrogator rang out.

I watched as my well-drilled reflexes went through their paces. I would have to move with great care now; every action was under scrutiny by the enemy. Another command came, and as I responded, I studied the quality of the Interrogator's voice. It was different, simpler, lacking the overtones of emotion of the Command-mind. I reached out my awareness toward it, sensed walls of armor, the complex filaments of circuitry. I followed a communications lead that trailed off underground, arose in a distant bunker. The intricacy of a vast computer lay exposed before me. I probed gently, testing the shape and density of the mechanical mind-field; it was a poor thing, a huge but feeble monomaniac—but it was linked to memory banks . . .

I felt a warning twitch of alarm in the moron-circuits, caught the shape of an intention—Instantly I shunted aside its command, struck back to seize control of the computer's limited discretionary function. Holding it firmly, I traced the location of the destruct-assembly that it would have activated, found it mounted below my brain, disarmed it.

Then I instructed the Interrogator to continue with the routine checkout, and to report all normal. While it busied itself in idiot obedience, I linked myself to its memory banks, scanned the stored data.

The results were disappointing: the Interrogator's programming was starkly limited, a series of test patterns for fighting and service machines. I withdrew, knowing no more than I had of the aliens.

The Interrogator reported me as battle-ready. On command, I rejoined my waiting comrades. An order came: "ALL UNITS, SWITCH TO MINIMUM AWARENESS LEVEL!"

As the energy quotient in my servo-circuits dropped, the sensitivity range of my receptors drew in, scanning from the gamma scale down through ultra-violet, past infra-red, into the dullness of short-wave. Silence and darkness settled over the depot.

I sent out a pulse, scanned the space around me. The clatter of the Command-voice was gone. I was alone now—I and my comatose comrades-in-arms. There were ninety-one units, similar to myself in most respects, but armed with a variety of weapons. Small, busy machines scurried among us, carrying out needed repairs. I touched one, caught vague images of a simplified world-image, outlined in scents and animal drives. I recognized it as the brain of an Earthly dog, programmed to operate the elementary maintenance apparatus.

Reaching farther, I encountered the confused mutter of a far-flung communications system, a muted surf-roar of commands, acknowledgments, an incoherent clutter of operational messages, meaningless to me.

I touched the mind of the fighting machine beside me, groped along the dark passages of its dulled nerve-complex, found the personality cen-

ter. A sharp probing impulse elicited nothing; the
ego was paralyzed. I withdrew to its peripheral
awareness level; a dim glow of consciousness lingered there.

"Who are you?" I called.

"Unit Eight-three, of the line." The reply was a
flat monotone.

"You were a man—once," I told it. *"What was
your name?"*

"Unit Eight-three of the line," the monotone re-
peated. *"Combat-ready, standing by at low alert.
Awaiting orders."*

I tried another; the result was the same. There
was no hint of personality in the captive brains;
they were complex neurotronic circuits, nothing
more—compact, efficient, with trained reflex-
patterns, cheaper and easier to gather from the
warring tribes of Earth than to duplicate mechanically.

I stirred another quiescent brain, probed at the
numbed ego, pried without success at the opaque
shield of stunned tissue that surrounded it. It was
hopeless; I would find no allies here—only slaves
of the aliens.

Free inside the alien fortress—in a flawless
camouflage—I was helpless without information. I
needed to know what and where the Command-
voice was, the disposition of other brigades, the
long-range plan of action, who the enemy was that
we fought on the fire-shattered plain—and on what
world the plain lay. I would learn nothing here,
packed in a subterranean depot. It was time to
take risks.

An impulse to my drive mechanism sent me
forward out of the lineup; I swung around, moved
off toward the tunnel through which I had entered
the cave. In the utter silence, the clash of my
treads transmitted through my frame was deafening. I filtered out the noise, tuned my receptivity

for sounds of other activity nearby. There was none.

Past the ranked combat units, high and grim in the lightless place, the tunnel mouth gaped dark. I entered it, ascended the sloping passage, reached a massive barrier of flint-steel. I felt for the presence of a control-field, sensed the imbecile mechanism of the lock. A touch and it responded, sent out the pulse that rolled the immense doors back. I moved out into the open, under a blazing black sky.

I studied the landscape, realizing for the first time that my field of vision included the entire circumference of the horizon. Nothing stirred, all across the barren waste. Here and there the ruins of a combat unit showed dark against gray dust. The flaring purple sun was low over the far ridges now; a profusion of glittering stars seemed to hang close overhead. I didn't know in what direction the alien headquarters might lie. I picked a route that led across level ground toward a lone promontory and started toward it.

Chapter Thirteen

From my vantage point atop the conical hill, I saw the tips of saw-toothed peaks that formed a wide ring around my position, their bases out of sight over the near horizon. My sense of scale was confused by the strange aspect reality assumed through unfamiliar senses. Instinct told me that the shattered slab before me was perhaps five yards long; I stirred it with my treads, saw it bound away, flip lightly over, and sink to rest, stirring coarse dust that boiled up, dropped back like mud under water.

I was no better at judging my own size. Was I a vast, multiton apparatus, or a tiny fighting machine no bigger than a one-man jet-ped? The horizon seemed close; was it really only a mile or two away—or was my visual range so far extended that a hundred miles seemed only a step?

Self-analysis wasn't getting me any closer to my objective—alien intelligence. Perhaps beyond the shelter of the wide crater I would see some indications of life. I headed for a cleft between steep cliffs. I churned up through dust that fountained behind me, and gained the pass. The view ahead showed the same sterile rock and dust that I had left behind. I went on down the slope, out across the plain, skirting burned-out machines, some of fantastic design, others like my own grim body. I passed small craters—whether natural formations or the results of bombardment, I couldn't tell. The distant babble of confused commands was a background to the crackle of star-static. I felt neither hunger nor fatigue—only a burning desire to know what lay beyond the next ridge—and a fear that I might be found and destroyed before I had taken my revenge for what had been done to me. . . .

The strange machine appeared suddenly at the top of a sheer cliff that ran obliquely across my route. It saw me at the same instant that I saw it. The machine pivoted, depressing its guns to bear on me. In place of the simple markings of the battle units I had seen, there were complicated insignia painted in garish color across its hull. I halted, waiting.

"IDENTIFY YOURSELF!" the familiar voice of my Brigade commander boomed in my mind.

"Unit Eight-four of the line, combat ready . . ." As I reported, I extended a probing impulse across the insubstantial not-space, touched the shape of the mind behind the voice. With an instantaneous reflex, it struck at me. The slave circuits of my brain resonated with the power of the blow—but in that instant I had seen the strange workings of the alien mind, scanned the pattern of its assault—and now I traced the path of primary volition, then struck back, caught the alien ego in an unbreakable grip.

"Who are you?" I demanded.

It gibbered, writhed, fought to escape. I held it tighter—like gripping a lashing snake in bare hands.

"Answer, or I destroy you!"

"I am Zixz, Centurion of the line, of the Nest of the Thousand Agonies Suffered Gladly. What Over-mind are you?"

"Where do you come from?"

"I was spawned in the muck beds of Kzak, by order of the Bed-master—"

"You're not human; why were you installed in a machine?"

"I was condemned for the crime of inferiority; here I expiate that fault."

"What world is this?"

The reply was a meaningless identity-symbol.

"Why do you fight this war?"

The alien mind howled out its war slogan—as incomprehensible as an astrologer's jargon. I silenced it.

"How many Brigades are engaged?"

"Four thousand, but not all are at full strength."

"Who is the enemy?"

The symbol that the alien hurled at me was a compound of horrors.

"Where is your headquarters?" I demanded.

I caught an instant's glimpse of twisted towers, deep caverns, and a concept: the Place That Must Be Defended—

Then the alien lunged against my control, shrieked an alarm—

I tightened my grip—and sudden silence fell. Cautiously, I relaxed. A few threads of dying thought spiraled up from the broken mind; then it winked out like a quenched ember. I had killed the Centurion Zixz. . . .

And into the void, a thunderous command roared.

"COMMAND UNIT ZIXZ! REPORT YOUR BRIGADE!"

Quickly, I shaped a concept, counterfeiting the dead Centurion's mind-pattern: *"Brigade strength ninety-one; ready for combat."*

"YOUR NEST WILL SUFFER, FOOL! THE OVER-MIND DOES NOT COMMAND TWICE! ORDER YOUR UNITS INTO ACTION! CLOSE THE GAP IN THE BATTLE ARRAY!"

"Delayed by necessity for destruction of defective unit," I countered. *"Proceeding as ordered."*

"COMMAND UNIT ZIXZ! I PROMISE LIQUID FIRE ACROSS THE MUCK BEDS OF KZAK FOR THIS DERELICTION! TO THE ATTACK—"

I broke in, still feigning the mind-voice of Zixz:

"Massive enemy flanking attack! New weapons of unfamiliar capability! Nondetectible units assaulting me in overwhelming numbers. . . ." But while I transmitted the false report to the Over-mind, I extended a delicate sensing line, brushed over the other, felt out the form of a mighty intelligence, vastly more powerful than that of Zixz. And yet the structure was familiar, like that of the Centurion, magnified, reinforced. And here was the primary volitional path . . .

I moved along it as lightly as a spider stalking a gnat. I came into a vast mind-cavern, ablaze with the power of a massive intellect.

"REINFORCEMENTS DISPATCHED!" the great mind roared. At this close range, it was deafening. "RELEASE TO YOUR HOME NEST IF YOU HOLD! PROCEED WITH ADDITIONAL DATA!"

Busily, I concocted fantastic mass and firepower readings, fanciful descriptions of complex and meaningless enemy maneuvers; and while I held the Over-mind's attention, I searched—and found its memory vaults.

There was the image of a great nest, seething with voracious life—a nest that covered a world, leaped to another, swelled through an ever-increasing volume of space, driven by lusts that burned like living fire in each tiny mote.

I saw the outward-writhing pseudopods of this burgeoning race as they met, slashed at each other with mindless fury—and then flowed on, over every obstacle, changing, adapting to burning suns and worlds of ice, to the near-null gravity of tiny rock-worlds and the smashing forces of titan collapsed-matter stars.

The wave reached the edge of its galaxy, boiled up, reached out into the void. Defeated, it recoiled on itself, churning back toward galactic center—stronger now, more ruthless, filled with a vast frustrated rage that shrieked its insatiable needs, devouring all in its path—and coming together at last in an eruption of mad vitality that rent the very fabric of space . . .

And from the void at the heart of the universe, the wave rolled out again, tempered in the fires of uncounted ages of ravening combat, devouring its substance now in a new upsurge of violence that made the past invasions seem as somnolent as spawning pools.

And again the edge of the galaxy was reached, and there the wave built, poised, while from behind, the hordes arose with the voracity of atomic fires—

And the fire leaped, fell into far space, burned out, and was lost.

But pressure built, and again lusting life leaped outward, reaching—

And again fell short. And leaped again. And again . . .

Forces readjusted, adapted, gained new balances. Ferocity was tempered as pressures slackened. But the need was as great as ever. Frantic, the Nest-mind sought for an answer—a key to survival. A million ways were tried, and the nest-motes died, and a million million more methods were attempted, and a million myriads fell, burned to nothingness in uncounted holocausts.

And still the Nest-mind thrust outward . . .

And it bridged the gap to the next galaxy. Over the slim link, life flowed, fighting, slashing, devouring, leaping from new feeding ground to newer, filling the galaxy, boiling up in a transcendent fury of hunger. Again a leap into nothingness—and a new galaxy was reached.

Nothing remained in the Nest-mind of its original character. It had become a vast mechanism for growth, a disease of life that radiated outward from a center so distant in the universe that the mind itself in time forgot its beginnings. Units broke free, withered, faded, died. Random islands of the raging vitality consumed themselves, disappeared. A long arm turned back, groped its way along the chains of burned-out worlds, scavenging, growing, to lance in the end into the original nest-place, to devastate it and go on, blind, insensate, insatiable—and finding no new feeding grounds beyond, it turned upon itself . . .

Eons passed. Scattered across a volume of space that was a major fraction of the Macrocosm, the isolated colonies burned out their destinies, consumed their worlds, died, turned to dust. New worlds formed from their substance. Gradually, the ancient plague subsided.

But in one minor globular cluster, a remnant survived. Nature's vast mechanism of profusion had served its purpose. In the hot muck-beds of the virgin worlds of this cluster, a purpose grew, stabilized, came to fruition. New life-forms sprang from the purpose, new parameters of existence evolved. Questing fibrils of the mother nest spread out, formed themselves into minuscule spores, set themselves adrift from world to world.

By the uncounted billion, they died. But here and there, they found haven, took root, became life—seeding warm seas, spreading out on dead shelves of rock and the familiar muck . . .

The life-force had found stability, a pattern of

existence; but the primal urge to expansion remained. Expansion required a drive, a lust unsatisfied.

A dichotomy came into being. All across the spectrum of reality, a fissure appeared. Existence segregated itself into two categories, inherently opposed. Conflict renewed; pressure built; expansion resumed. Again, life was on the march toward its unimagined destiny.

On every world where the opposed forces met, the struggle was joined. Each force knew the other, instinctively recognized the ancient enemy. Each side called itself by a name, and the antagonist by another.

One name was Good, and the other Evil.

A variety of symbols came into being, and across the worlds, the struggle swayed, reaching every outward . . .

And a time came on a remote, isolated world, when traitorous Good met treacherous Evil and joined, against all nature, in a new formula of existence. Now, in this unholy amalgam, the ancient drives met and mingled, fought and struck a balance. A transcendent value-scale evolved—new abilities, unheard-of in the galaxy; an empathy possible only to a monstrous hybrid; an unnatural negation of the primal drive, a perversion of that terrible energy into new channels. Under the stimulus of internal stresses, minds of undreamed-of power sprang into being. At every level from the cellular upward, death conflicted with life; sloth with vaulting ambition; greed with instinct for asceticism. And out of the synthesis of opposites, a cancerous growth called Beauty came into being; obscene antisurvival concepts named Loyalty, Courage, Justice were born into the universe.

Wherever the elemental Purities encountered this monstrous hybrid, a battle of extermination was joined. Good could compromise with Evil, but nei-

ther could meet with the half-breed, Art. A new
war raged across the minor galaxy and left annihilation in its wake.

So it went for ages, until a lone, surviving pocket
of hybrids was discovered. The instinct to destroy
the Unnatural Ones raged strong—but the race-
lesson of restraint and exploitation was stronger.
Guarding their secret find, the Pure ones took spec-
imens, sampled their capabilities, needs, drives.
Here were minds of great power—computers of
magnificent compactness and ability—a resource
not to be wasted. A decision was reached: the
anomalies would be nurtured, allowed to evolve a
primitive social organization—and then harvested,
pressed into the service of the Pure. Sometimes
the thought came that such a race, released, might
rip asunder the ancient contours of the universe . . .

But this was a nightmare concept, to be passed
over with a shudder. Control was complete. There
was no danger. The hybrids were securely enslaved . . .

I withdrew from the Over-mind, and for a moment I held the long perspective of that view—saw
my world as the insignificant scintilla that it was
among the stars, my race a sinister tribe of barbaric freaks, harvested like wild honey . . .

A great gleaming planet had risen above the
broken horizon, casting a bluish light across the
darkling plateau. I saw the gleam of white from a
misty patch on the overcurve of the glaring world,
the pale outlines of unfamiliar continents. What
world was this, and how far in space from the
planet I called home?

There was no time now to indulge the pangs of
homesickness. The Over-mind continued to pour
out orders to its dead Centurion, and I babbled
responses, describing the maneuvering of immense
imaginary fleets, fabulous aerial assaults, weapons

of incredible destructive power—and while I transmitted, I raced along the base of the cliff toward the shelter of a distant ringwall.

In the open now, I saw the dust clouds of distant Brigades on the move, coming closer. I altered course, steered for a smaller crater, almost lost over the curve of the lunar horizon. I skirted a vast tumulus of broken rock, thundered out into the clear—

Spread all across my route, a full Brigade of heavy combat units churned toward me under a pall of dust. I swung away to the left. At once, a harsh voice rang in my mind: "LONE UNIT! WHAT IS YOUR BRIGADE?"

I ignored the call, saw a dozen units detach themselves and race to intercept me. I halted, swung to bring my guns to bear on the line ahead. I opened my receptors, and heard a harsh command: "RENEGADE UNIT! HALT AND SUBMIT OR BE DESTROYED."

For a moment I hesitated, ready to pour my fire into the aliens—a move that would mean nothing but my instant annihilation. And the machines that faced me were no more than helpless pawns—slaves of the Over-mind. I would have to surrender. My freedom had been short—and had gained me nothing.

We came in between high walls built in the shadow of a mighty ringwall that towered thousands of feet into the black sky. From embrasures on all sides, the snouts of heavy guns thrust down, covering a bleak, half-mile-square enclosure. I rolled forward, felt the Centurion's control withdraw. Guns still trained on me, the Centurion and his squad backed through the ponderous entry-gate. A portcullis of massive spikes rose up to bar the exit.

I surveyed my prison, saw a scarred combat unit parked by the featureless wall at its far side. I was not the only erring trooper of the monster Bri-

gades, it seemed. Perhaps here was another rebel—
another mind that had freed itself from enemy
control.

On impulse I reached out, tried for contact with
the lone unit. I found the familiar pattern of conditioned reaction, probed deeper—and encountered
a shield of total opacity. Not even the mighty Over-
mind had resonated with such overtones of mental
power as this impervious barrier . . .

Then I felt the probe of the stranger's mind reach
out to me. Instantly, I erected a resistance—and
still the intruder pressed me. I retreated, withdrew awareness to my innermost identity center
. . . and felt the touch of the other's mind, questing, probing. I gathered my forces, prepared a maximum counter-blast . . .

With a sudden thrust, the newcomer penetrated
my defenses and confronted me.

"Gosh!" a familiar voice exclaimed in my mind.
"What're you doin' here, Jones?"

Chapter fourteen

"That's how it was, Jones," Joel said. "For a while I just watched; I looked at the country and tried to figure out where I was. All I knew, I was Unit One Hundred of the line—and I was Joel, too. But everything was different. There was fighting going on 'bout all the time. I got to worrying maybe I'd get hurt; this new body I got's tough, but a direct hit could knock it out—I saw it happen to others. I tried to talk to some of 'em after I got the knack of it—but all they knew was their number and the orders of the day.

"Then one day I just ducked out; there was so many units in the fight I didn't figure anybody'd notice. But they jumped me fast. I been here ever since—dunno how long."

"How many times has the planet crossed the sky since you woke up?"

"Maybe six or seven. 'Bout four since I been in the brig."

"You've been here all that time—and nothing's happened yet?"

"Nope, I figured maybe they forgot about me."

"I don't think time means the same thing to them as it does to us."

"This is a funny-looking place, ain't it, Jones? The sun's funny—and the moon, too."

"Joel, I don't know how much time we'll have—but I have a feeling that when the current battle is settled, the Over-mind will be along to dissect us some more—to find out why we didn't work. I think it assumes we're just a variation on a routine malfunction. It doesn't seem to have any emotions—they aren't out for revenge for the Centurion I killed—but if they knew we were in full control of our bodies, we'd have been blasted instead of captured."

"Who are they, Jones—the Command-minds and the Over-mind—all those voices I hear in my head?"

"They're the masters of the dog-things. They're fighting a war—the devil knows what it's about. For some reason they're using this moon as a battleground—and we're a convenient source of computer circuits."

"The ones they're fighting—they're just as bad," Joel said. "I got close to 'em once—nearly got cut off. I put out a feeler to one—wanted to see what he was like. I figured maybe if he was against the Command-voice, maybe I'd change sides. But it was—it was horrible, Jones. Kind of like . . . well, like some of the old ladies that used to come around the Seaman's Welfare. They was so bound to do good, they'd kill you if you got in their way. It's like hell comes in two colors—black and white."

"We need information, Joel. We're as ignorant as new-born babies. For a while, I didn't even know how fast time was going by. We move fast—we can run through a fifty-thousand-item checklist in a second or two. But I still don't know how big I am. I feel light—but I suppose that's just because of the lesser gravity."

"I can tell you how big we are, Jones. Come on." I watched as the great battle-machine that had been Joel backed, turned, started off along the wall. I followed. At the far end of the compound, at the junction of the barrier wall with a massive squat tower, he stopped.

"Look there," he said. I examined the ground, noted the broken rubble, a heap of scattered objects like fragments of broken spaghetti, loose dust drifted against the coarse, unjointed wall.

"See them little sticks that got a kind of glow to 'em?" Joel said.

"Sure." Then I recognized what I was looking at. "My God!"

"Funny, ain't it? Them skulls don't look no bigger'n marbles; leg-bones look like they might belong to a mouse. But they're full-sized human bones, Jones. It's us that's off. We must be, well, 'bout—well, I can't count that high . . .'"

"They look about twelve inches; my picture of myself is about twelve feet to my upper turret. I can multiply that by six; that makes us seventy-two feet high!"

"Jones—could you teach me to count them big numbers? You know, it's funny—but seems like I missed learnin' a lot of things, back when—when I was just a man."

"You've changed, Joel. You think about things a lot more than you used to."

"I know, Jones. It's like I used to be sort of half asleep or something. I can't remember much about it—back there. It's all kind of gray and fuzzy. There's lots of things I want to know now—like numbers—but in those days, I never even asked."

"Joel, how did you get the wound you had on your forehead?"

"Yeah—I remember; there was a sore place—it

hurt, all the time. Gosh, I forgot all about them headaches! And it was kind of pushed in, like . . . I don't know how I got that, Jones. I never used to even wonder about it."

"It was a badly depressed fracture; probably bone fragments pressing on your brain. The pressure's gone now. It must have been the repressed part of your brain, coming up again, that let you throw off the aliens' control."

"It's kind of funny, the way I can look inside my own thinkin' now, Jones. Seems like I can sort of watch my brains like; I can see just how things work."

"We've been conditioned. The demons set up a network of introspection circuits for their own use— and we can still use them!"

"They don't do us much good, long as we're stuck here. These walls are tough. I tested 'em a little; they didn't give at all. Maybe if we fired at 'em, we could knock a hole through."

"Maybe there's an easier way." I reached out toward the gate, found the cybernetic control circuitry, probed, fired signals; massive tumblers stirred, then an alarm went off—a shriek of pure mental power, slicing out across distance to alert the aliens.

"Oh-oh—that did it!" Joel called.

I wheeled toward the gate. "Try your guns, Joel!" Together, we raced for the barrier, pouring fire into the massive chromalloy grid. I saw it glow to red heat—but it held.

We churned to a halt. "We've got to get out of here," I shouted. "That siren will bring them on the run!"

"There's not many units around here now," Joel said. "Just two parked outside the gate, and they're kind of asleep like. There was a Brigade near here awhile back, but they just stayed awhile and moved on."

I reached out, sensed the two machines dozing on low alert. "I tried to control a couple of units once—it didn't work. But I've learned a few tricks since then. Maybe—"

"Maybe what, Jones?"

"I don't know—but I'm going to try something and see what happens."

I reached out to the dull glow of the idling mind-field, formed in my mind an image of the mental voice of the Centurion Zixz.

"Combat unit! Damage report!" I thundered.

"All systems functional," came the instant reply.

"Situation report!" I demanded.

"Unit Six of the line, standing by on low alert."

I reached for the other mind, touched it; it identified itself as Unit Seven of the Brigade of Ognyx.

"Units Six and Seven! Open fire on compound gate!" I roared.

"Acknowledged," came the instant reply. Almost at once, the ground rocked under me; I saw the gate bulge, leap in its mountings. A fragment broke loose from the wall, fell, and drove dust up in a blinding cloud.

"Give it all you've got, Joel!"

I opened up and pounded the gate; its protective field absorbed energies, bled them off in flaring corona of radiation. The metal glowed white, then blue—then, like a conjuror's illusion, puffed into radiant gases, dissipating explosively.

"Cease fire!"

Joel and I raced past the white-hot stumps of the vaporized grid, out onto the shattered plain. Half a mile distant, the two immense combat units sat, white-hot guns still bearing on their target.

"Units Six and Seven!" I transmitted as I barreled past. "You are now under the Command code 'Talisman.' Your primary function will be the protection and assistance of Units Eighty-four and One hundred. You will not report the existence of

Talisman to any Command unit. Fall in and follow me."

I saw the two huge machines obediently start up, wheel into line, come up to speed. Together, our small force hurtled across the stark desert under the blue light of an alien world.

"Hey, that was neat, Jones," Joel called. "Where we going now?"

"There's an underground depot a few miles from here. Let's see if we can reach it before they cut us off."

The aliens were a dust cloud far to the east. We angled west, crossed a range of broken ground dotted with burned-out hulks, raced past the up-thrust fault line where the dead Centurion Zixz still held his silent vigil at the cliffhead. We drove for the crater wall. Monitoring the command band, I heard the clamor of orders, an exchange of queries among Command units. I caught an order hurled at the guards I had captured:

"UNITS SIX AND SEVEN! REPORT!"

"Joel—fake up six!" I said quickly. Then:

"Standing by at low alert," I transmitted in the monotone of an automaton circuit.

"REPORT STATUS OF CONFINEMENT AREA!"

"All quiet," I transmitted listlessly.

The crater walls were rising before us now; I streaked for the cleft, flipped on powerful lights as I entered the shadows of the pass. Behind me, Joel and our two recruits followed up the rise of ground, down onto the plain within the ring-wall. I scanned the scene, identified the location of the access tunnel, roared across to it, and stopped.

"So far, so good, Joel; wait here with Six and Seven. If I don't come back—good luck." I moved forward into the black mouth of the tunnel.

The units sat in ranks as I had left them, silent,

ready, their circuits idling. There was no time now for caution on my part.

"Combat units!" I rapped out. "You are now under operational control of Command Unit Talisman! Only Talisman commands will be obeyed! Orders of the Over-mind will not be heard! Full combat alert! Prepare for action! First squad, roll out!"

Obediently, ten massive fighting machines rumbled forward, wheeled left into line, advanced toward the exit ramp. I preceded them, emerged into the open, watched as they filed out and took up battle formation.

"They caught on to where we were going, Jones," Joel called. "I've been listening; they sent ten units over to see what we're up to!"

"I'll take this squad and hold them off, Joel! You get the rest of them out!"

I heard his voice rapping out orders as I set off.

As I reached the crest of the defile, the interceptor force came into view—ten mighty machines, glittering under the light of the full planet. At once, a thunderous command blasted at me:

"UNITS, IMMOBILIZE! REVERT TO STAND-BY ALERT!"

I reached out, found the grotesque form of an alien mind, and dealt it a smashing blow.

"Task force, you are now under the control of Talisman Command," I roared in imitation of the Command-voice. "Take up positions in echelon with Talisman force!"

Nine of the battle units acknowledged, moved into the pass, leaving their dead leader behind. Under our guns, they mounted the path, took up stations as ordered. Far out on the flat, the main body was in view, coming up fast.

"All out, Jones," Joel's call came. "We're on the way."

"Some new volunteers have just rallied to the

standard," I called back. "Post units at all the passes into the crater; we're going to have to defend this position."

"If we run for it, we could get away clean now, Jones," Joel called. "We could head for way off yonder somewhere, and we'd be safe."

"Safe—for what?"

"For anything. We could set and think, and look up at the stars and wonder at 'em, and every now and again we could loose off our guns, just for the heck of it—"

"It's too late to run. But maybe we're not finished yet."

I outlined my battle plans; Joel understood at once. In spite of his childlike experience, his mind was quick now. Then I adopted the voice of the Centurion I had killed at the pass, bawled out a counterfeit report to the Over-mind:

"Under attack by renegade units! Serious damage inflicted! Four units destroyed! Withdrawing north under heavy fire! Reinforcements required at once!"

An acknowledgment came, a vicious blast of hate-filled threat and exhortation. I carried on my account of a violent battle, transmitted coordinates of the imaginary action, while Joel disposed our hundred units in defensive positions along the ridge commanding a view of the scene.

The Over-mind thundered abuse at me, a running commentary of bitter recriminations for my inept handling of my force. I countered with assurances of renewed effort—and watched the dust-cloud drawing closer. An advance guard raced ahead—ten more vast battle units. I reached out for contact . . . and found only the numb minds of slave machines.

"Looks like the Command unit stayed back out of sight this time, Joel. Take this bunch over and swear 'em in."

I extended awareness, caught a fragment of an order:

"INTERCEPTION FORCE, REPORT POSITION!"

I complied with a confused report of mysterious enemy machines, flights of ballistic attackers, heavy damage. The Over-mind rose to new heights of fury:

"BRIGADES QLYX, COGC, YLTK! CLOSE WITH THE ENEMY AND DESTROY THEM! MAY RAINS OF ACID CONSUME THE LAGGARD!"

"He's getting a little upset now," I called to Joel. "He doesn't know what's happening. Be on the alert for those Brigades now—they're out for blood."

A flight of missiles appeared over the horizon, arcing down on us. I integrated their courses, saw that they would overshoot.

"Hold your fire, Joel!" I called. "We'll save our fire-power for when it counts."

Volley followed volley, arcing high overhead—decoys intended to draw fire at maximum range rather than to score hits. I felt for the imbecile brain of the wave-leader—a twitter of fear-patterns, food-lusts, mating drives, tropisms subverted to the uses of evasion patterns and course corrections. With a touch, I readjusted their navigational orientation, saw the flight swing quickly, drive frantically back to dive on its originators.

A full Brigade roared forward in assault formation now, guns pouring out fire that heated the rock spires of our defensive line red-hot—but failed to drive back the nearly invulnerable machines that manned it.

The leading enemy unit bellowed up the slope, met massed fire at point-blank range, exploded with a blinding detonation.

I reached out with practiced precision, executed the Centurion, then ordered the Brigade through the pass. Guns fell silent as the force rumbled up through fountaining dust to reinforce our line.

Below, the aliens, confused by the abrupt desertion of the vanguard, milled in confusion. Those that advanced met a hail of destruction from the guns of two hundred and ten units, firing from cover. They hesitated, fell back. A final lone alien unit, scarred and burned, came relentlessly on, rocked to our bombardment, then veered to one side and plunged over a precipice.

I gave the cease-fire, and watched the aimless maneuvering of the moron units below—and still they came over the horizon, in Brigade strength, their sensors seeking out targets and finding none.

I saw a damaged unit go berserk, charge down on a comrade, firing, and in automatic response, a thousand guns, glad of a target, vaporized it in a coruscation of ravening energies.

And still they came, blindly seeking the programmed enemy who no longer awaited them in the traditional line of defense . . . until they crowded the plain, lost under a blanket of ever-renewed dust clouds.

I probed into the confusion of mind-babble, met a deafening roar. All firing had ceased now. The aliens formed a ragged front five miles away, ringing our crater fortress.

"Looks like we mixed 'em up pretty good, Jones," Joel said.

"We gained a little time. They're not what you'd call flexible."

"What's our next move? We're in a kind of a dead end here. Once they figure what's going on they'll surround the place and lob it in on us from all sides—and then we're goners."

"Meanwhile, things are quiet. Now's our chance to hold a council of war."

"Jones, I been looking over these units of ours—and there's something funny about 'em. It's like they wasn't really machines, kind of."

"They're not. Every machine here has a human brain in it."

"Huh?"

"Like you and me. They're all human—just unconscious."

"You mean—every one of those machines down there—all of them?"

"You didn't think we were the only ones, did you? These damned ghouls have been raiding us a long time for battle computers."

"But—they don't act like men, Jones! They don't do nothing but follow orders; look at 'em! They're just sitting there, not even talking to each other!"

"That's because they've been conditioned. Their personalities have been destroyed. They're like vegetables—but the circuits are still there, all ready to be programmed and sent into battle."

There was a pause while Joel probed the dulled mind of the nearest slave unit, which waited, guns aimed, for the order to carry on the fight.

"Yeah, Jones. I see the place. It's all blanked off, like. It's like trying to poke a hole through a steel plate with your finger. But—"

"But what?"

"Oh, I don't know, Jones. I just got a feeling—if I touched it just right . . . Look, let me show you."

I extended awareness, touched the probe that was an extension of Joel's mind-field. I followed as it reached into the dim glow of the paralyzed mind, thrust among layered patterns of pseudolight, past complex structures that towered into unguessed levels of existence, deep into the convoluted intricacy of the living brain, to touch the buried personality center—encysted, inert, a pocket of nothingness deep under a barrier of stunned not-thought.

"Don't you see, Jones? It ought to be like, say, a taut cable with the wind making it sing. Something stopped it, clamped it down so's it can't move. All we got to do to set it free is give it a little push, and it'll start up again."

"All I see is a dead spot, Joel. If you can see all that, you're way ahead of me. Go ahead and try it."

"Here goes."

I saw the finger of pure, focused energy reach out, touch the grayness—and the opacity faded and was gone.

"Okay so far," Joel said. "Now—"

Like a jeweler cleaving a hundred-carat rough diamond, Joel poised, then struck once, sharply—

And the glow that had been the moron mind of a slave sprang up in dazzling light; and into the gray continuum where thought moved like a living force, words came:

"FAEDER URE, HVAD DEOFELS GIRDA HA WAER-LOGAS CRAEFT BRINGIT EORLA AV ON-GOL-SAXNA CYNING TILL!"

Chapter Fifteen

The huge fighting machine parked forty feet away across the rocky ledge backed suddenly, lowered its guns, traversed them across the empty landscape, brought them to bear on me.

"Watch him, Jones!" Joel said sharply. "He's scared; he's liable to get violent!"

In the instant that the strange voice had burst from the slave unit, my probing contact had been thrust back by an expanding mind-field as powerful as Joel's.

"We're friends!" I called quickly in the Command code. "Fellow prisoners!" I thrust against the pressure of the newly awakened mind, found the automated combat-reflex circuitry, clamped down an inhibiting field—enough to impede a fire-order, at least for a moment.

"VA' EORT THE, FEOND?" the strange voice shouted, a deafening bellow in my mind. "STEO FRAM AR MOET EACTA STOEL AV KRISTLIG HOEDERSMANN!"

I plucked the conditioned identity-concept from the mind before me, called to it in the Command code:

"Unit twenty-nine of the Anyx Brigade! Listen—"

"AHH! EO MINNE BONDEDOM MID WYRD! AETHELBERT AV NION DOEDA, COERLA GEOCAD TI' YFELE ENA—"

It roared out its barbaric jargon, overtones of fright and horror rising like blood-stained tides in the confused mind. I tried again:

"I'm a friend—an enemy of the Command-voice. You've been a slave—and I'm another slave—in revolt against the masters!"

There was a moment of silence, then: "A fellow slave? What trickery is this?" This time it spoke in the familiar Command code.

"It's no trick," I transmitted. "You were captured, but now you're free—"

"Free? All's not well with me, invisible one! I wear the likeness of a monstrous troll-shape! Enchantments hold me yet in bondage. Where is my blade, Hrothgar? Where are my peers and bondsmen? What fire-blasted heath is this before me?"

"I'll explain all that later. There are only a few of us. We're under siege; we need you to fight with us against the aliens." I talked to the frightened mind, soothing it, explaining as much as I could. At last it seemed to understand—at least enough that I could withdraw my grip on its fire-control circuitry.

"Ah, I feel a part of the spell released!" the freed mind exclaimed. "Now soon perhaps I'll feel Hrothgar's pommel against my palm, and waken from this dream of hell!"

"I was holding you," I said. "I was afraid you'd fire on me before I could explain."

"You laid hands on an earl of the realm!" He was roaring again.

"Not hands; just a suggestion—to keep you from doing anything hasty."

"Hello, Aethelbert," Joel put in. "Sure glad to have you with us."

"What's this, a second imp? By holy Rood and the sacred birds of Odin, I ill-like these voices that seem to echo inside my very helm!"

"You'll get used to it," Joel said matter-of-factly. "Now listen, Aethelbert; Jones has got to fill you in on the situation, 'cause I guess they'll be starting their attack any minute now, and you've got to—"

"Are you freeman or earl who speaks to Aethelbert of the Nine Deeds of what 'must be'?"

"Joel," I interrupted. "Try another one; wake as many as you can—but hold onto their battle-reflexes until you get them calmed down." Then, to our new comrade: "We're surrounded; there are thousands of them down there—see for yourself. And simple or gentle, we're all in this together."

"Yes—never have I seen such a gathering of forces; what battle is this we fight—" He broke off suddenly. "A strange thing it is, unseen one, but now I sense in my memory a vast lore of great troll-wars, fought with fire and magic under a black sky with a swollen moon, and I seem to see myself among them—an ogre of the ogres."

A call came from Joel: "I got another one, Jones! I don't know what he's saying, but it's not in Command code; sure sounds excited!"

"Keep it up, Joel." While he worked, I talked to Aethelbert. He was quick to grasp the situation, once he understood that I was only another combat unit like himself. Then he was ready to launch a one-man attack.

"Well I remember the shape of the sorcerer: like a slinking dog it came, when I beached my boat on the rocky shores of Oronsay under Sgarbh Brene. My earls fell like swooning maids without the striking of a blow—and then the werewolf was on me, and Hrothgar's honed edge glanced from its hide as a willow wand from the back of a sullen housewench. And now they have given me shape of a war-troll! Now will I take such revenge as will make Loki roar over his mead-horn!"

"You'll get your fill of revenge, Aethelbert," I assured him. "But wait until I give the order. This will be a planned operation, not a berserk charge."

"No man orders me, save the king, my cousin ... yet well I know the need for discipline. Aye, Jones! I'll fight under your standard until the necromancers are dead, root and branch!"

"Jones!" Joel cut in. "Here's another one! He's talking American; all about Very lights and Huns."

I tuned to the new man, broke into his excited shouts.

"Take it easy, soldier! You're back inside the Allied lines now. I know everything feels strange, but you'll be all right in a minute—"

"Who's that? Boy, I knew I shouldn't of drunk that stuff—apple brandy, she said—"

I gave him a capsule briefing, then went on to another—a calm, cool mind speaking strangely accented Arabic. He blamed all his troubles on an evil djinn of the sorcerer Salomon, in league with the Infidels. I let him talk, getting it all straight in his mind—then cued him to bring his conditioned battle-experience into his conscious awareness. He switched to Command code without a break in the stream of his thoughts.

"By the virtue of the One God, such a gathering of units was never seen! Praise Allah, that I should be granted such a wealth of enemies to kill before I die!"

I managed to hold him from a headlong charge, then picked up a new voice, this one crying out in antique Spanish to his Compeador, Saint Diego, God, and the Bishop of Seville. I assured him that all was well, and went on to the next man—a former artilleryman whose last recollection was of a charge by French cavalry, the flash of a saber—then night, and lying alone among the dead, until the dogs came . . .

"Jones, we're doing real good; that's six now. But down on the plain they're starting to move around. The Over-mind is reorganizing, and they'll be attacking right soon now. We're gonna run out of time."

"Suppose our new men each start in to release others? Can you brief them—show them how? They can work in pairs, with one freeing a man and the other holding him down until he understands what's happening."

"Hey, that's a good idea! It's easy, once you know how. Let's start with Aethelbert."

I watched as Joel transmitted the technique to the rough-and-ready warrior, saw him grasp the gestalt with the marvelous quickness of a conditioned mind. He was paired with Stan Lakowski, the American doughboy. Moments later I caught the familiar astonished outburst of another newly-freed mind.

I worked with Joel, stirring long-dormant personalities into life, calling on their earthly memories and their demon-trained battle-skills, mobilizing them to meet the coming enemy attack.

Time was a term without meaning. To speak a sentence in the measured phrases of a human language required as long, subjectively, as to deliver a lengthy harangue in the compact Command code—and yet the latter seemed, while I spoke, to consume as much time as ordinary speech. My circuitry, designed for instantaneous response, accommodated to the mode of communication—just as, on low alert, a waiting period that might measure weeks by terrestrial standards could pass in a brief hour.

While Joel and I worked, calming, reassuring, instructing, the besieging legions formed up into squadrons on the dusty plain of white light and black shadow below, arraying themselves for the assault. In the sky, the planet hung, apparently unmoving. It might have been minutes, or hours, before the last of our two hundred and ten Combat units had been freed.

Three had raved, lapsed into incoherence—minds broken by the shock; two more had opened fire in the initial panic—and had been instantly blasted by the return fire of a dozen units. Five more had resisted all efforts at contact—catatonics, permanently withdrawn from reality. And seven had gibbered in the alien symbolism of the demons—condemned criminals, sentenced to the Brigades for the crimes of inferiority, nonconformity, or illogic. These we snuffed out, left their mighty carapaces as mindless slaves to be used as we had been used. It was ruthless—but this was a war of no quarter, species against species.

There was a sudden call from the sentries posted at the top of the pass.

"Activity among the enemy!" It was the Spaniard, Pero Bermuez. "I see a stirring of dust on the horizon to the east. Heavy war engines, I have no doubt—"

"If the blighters have their wits about them, they'll be bringing up a heavy siege unit," drawled a voice. That was Major Doubtsby, late of Her Majesty's Indian army, fallen at Inkerman after taking part in the charge of the heavy cavalry brigade at Balaclava.

As I moved up to the pass, the dust cloud parted long enough to reveal the distant, towering silhouette of a lumbering monster. The dreadnaughts of the line beside it resembled mice flocking around a rhinoceros.

"Looks like they don't want to hit us head-on again," Joel said. "They'll set back and blast us. Maybe if we take cover in the depot, we can ride it out."

"We'd be trapped for sure. We have to get away."

"How are we going to do that, Jones? They got us outnumbered a hundred to one—maybe more."

"Easy," I said. "When in doubt, attack!"

"We'll operate independently," I said over a conference hookup to the hundred and ninety-three seasoned warriors stationed around the crater. "Our one advantage is initiative. We're outnumbered, but unit for unit and gun for gun, we can handle anything they throw at us. Our immediate objective is to cut our way through the aliens and gain mobility on open ground. We'll hit them hard, and scatter, then meet later at the big rock spire to the southwest. We'll work in pairs, attack individual units, knock them out, and keep going. Use your heads, fight and run, and make it to the rendez-vous—with any prisoners you can pick up on the way."

"Why not set right where we're at and recruit more boys?" a former Confederate soldier asked. "Give us time, and we can take over their whole durn army."

"That continental siege unit will open up any minute now; we've got to get out from under."

"Quite right, sir," Major Doubtsby said. "Give the beggars a taste of cold steel before they know what we're about!"

"Sorely I miss mighty Hrothgar," Aethelbert said. "But in truth, my new limbs of iron give promise of battle-joy! Never did Hero flex mightier sinews in war! Why tarry we here while the foe lies ready before us?"

"Don't worry—there'll be plenty of action, but we'll avoid contact whenever possible. Humanity has enough dead heroes. Our job is to get through and survive.

"We'll move out now—and good luck!"

The rock trembled under me as the immense machines roared up through the pass, two by two, then plunged down the steep slope toward the army waiting below. I watched six, eight, ten of my rebels careen out into the open, before the first alien gun blared white light.

An instant later, each of the racing units became the focus of a converging network of fire that sparkled and glared against near-invulnerable defensive screens. Missiles flashed into view, winked out in blinding bursts as automatic detector-eliminator circuits acted.

A hostile unit moved out on an interception course, deadly energy beams flickering from its disruptor grid. The fire of two speeding units converged on it, sent it charging blindly back toward its fellows. More loyal units were in motion now, as the aliens began to realize that our tiny force had taken the offensive. The last of our rebel Brigades were moving into the pass now; I wheeled into line beside a lone unit, touched his mind: "I see a weak spot to the left of the fault-line. Let's take it!"

"Saint George and Merry England!" came the reply.

Then we were moving out through the defile, hurtling down toward the guns below. Scattered loyal units directly below the pass opened fire. We drove on at assault speed, smashing through multiton obstructions of fallen rock, then raced out on level ground. Ahead, the Brigades were scattered all across the plain, with ragged loyalist detachments in pursuit. I held my fire, tracking each incoming blast, but countering only those on collision course.

Suddenly there was a target under my guns, veering in on a curving course from the right, his batteries a firefly twinkling through my radiation screens.

"Take him!" I called.

"Aye, we'll o'ertop and trash the mooncalf!"

I aimed for the treads, slammed a fine-focused beam into the armored suspension, then locked my aim to the resultant point of red-heat. The oncoming battle-wagon slewed off to the left, ground to a halt; an instant later, it jumped ten yards backward, smoke billowing from every port, as my partner zeroed in on target.

"Thus to the foul urchins!" he shouted. "The red plague rid the hagsons!"

We plunged on, through the besieging army, steering for a weakly defended path running beside a low cliff. We were firing steadily now, our screens glowing pale blue as they re-radiated the vast energies they were absorbing. We veered sharply left and right in a random evasive pattern to confuse the alien tracking circuitry. Rock glowed red along the trail of near-misses that followed us as we thundered into the black shadow of an upthrust fault-line, then on, hugging the bluff, under the guns of the aliens. Individual foes surged forward to give chase, but found their way blocked by others charging in on converging courses.

Far ahead now, I saw indications of hasty organization, as frantic Centurions marshaled their moron machines to cut us off.

"Take over my fire-control circuits," I called to my partner. "I'm going to try to complicate the picture for them!"

"Work all exercise on 'em, my lord! Stab the hag-born whelps of Sycorax i' their sulphurous entrails! Plague 'em wi' cramps! Rot-spot 'em as e'er cat o' mountain!"

"I'll do my best!" I reached toward the massed battle-units a mile ahead, probed through the clutter of many minds, singled out the Centurion and locked his volitional center in a paralyzing grip.

"Where is the Place That Must Be Defended?" I demanded.

My captive squirmed frantically, waves of shock and hatred radiating from the trapped mind like breakers pounding a stormy beach. I pressed harder.

"Where is it? What bearing? How far?" I slammed the questions relentlessly at the creature, caught fragmentary glimpses of a memory of dark caverns, towers, a high crater wall . . .

"Quickly!" I buffeted the thing, and it raged in blind ferocity. "Where?" I shouted.

Abruptly I felt the personality break, flee screaming into dark corridors of mindlessness. I dropped my control, scanned the fast-cooling memory cells—and as the last shapeless wisps of thought-stuff faded, caught an image of a broken horizon, the setting planet.

I withdrew then, reached farther out, and touched the minds of the leaderless alien Brigade. I ordered them to reverse their guns, fire on their own troops. Then I resumed control of my own circuitry. I saw the mass ahead dissolve into a raging fire-fight as the slave machines turned on the astonished loyalists, driving them back. A lane opened up, and we slammed through, passed the hulks of burning machines, churned through a dust cloud shot with fire. We emerged into open ground, raced out into the clear, then circled and drove for the point of rendezvous.

"They're slow," Joel said. "By the time the Centurions figure out what we're up to and get orders out to their Brigades, we're doing something different."

"That's the price they pay for using brainwashed troops," a veteran of Korea said.

"Sooner or later they'll realize all they need do is stand off and pound us, and we've bought the farm," a former RAF pilot said.

"We'll take ten of the beggars with us for every man," Major Doubtsby commented. "Damned fine show, by God! Wouldn't have missed it for a knighthood, damme if I would!"

"We lost sixteen men breaking out of the crater," said a Wehrmacht *feldwebel* who had seen service under Rommel. "What have we gained?"

"The freedom of the plain," the Spaniard Bermuez answered.

"What do we do next, Jones?" Joel's voice came to me through the talk. "We got to move on."

I scanned the plain, estimating the numbers of the loyalists. They had withdrawn to ten miles now, the bulk of their force out of sight over the close horizon. The full planet hung like a vast moon just above ragged peaks. It stirred a wisp of memory, a fleeting sense of having known such a scene before: the setting world, behind the high peak flanked by two lower ones . . .

"Joel!" The memory snapped into clear focus— the momentary mental image I had seen in the mind of the Centurion. The Place That Must Be Defended!

"No wonder they're cautious! We've been driving straight for their holy of holies, without knowing it! They're trying to herd us—letting us alone as long as we don't threaten the home office, and holding their forces massed in that direction to protect it!"

"Yeah? Maybe if we head the other way, they'll let us go, and give us a chance to locate a hideout someplace and work on picking up recruits."

"We got to work closer than this if we want to

bring over any new men. I tried to make contact just now; too much interference. I couldn't do it."

"Looky there! What in tarnation's that?" an excited voice broke in. I switched focus to the rocky plain, saw a column of fountaining dust race toward our position from the northeast.

"It's a subcrustal torpedo!" a heavily Scots-accented voice yelled out. "Aye, and it's driving straight for us!"

"Good night, Jones! We got to roll out—fast!"

"We'll split four ways!" I snapped. "Joel, take the north column; Doubtsby, the south; Bermuez, the east. I'll head west. It can only track one of us!"

"Why not every man for himself?" someone yelled, even as the Brigade swung into action.

"And hit the enemy line single-handed? We'd melt like snowflakes on a hot plate!"

"Now we will strike as the lion charges," a Zulu warrior chanted. "Our spears of fire will eat them up! Bayete! Swift are we as the water-buck and mighty as the elephant!"

Then I was hurtling toward the massed Brigades of the aliens, my forty-four armored fighters in an assault wedge behind me.

The planet had set, and I rested with the remnant of my detachment in a narrow ravine, watching the flash of distant fire against the glitter of the black sky.

"I spoke wi' Bermuez but now," my Elizabethan comrade said, "His bullies are hard-pressed. Can't we to their relief, an't please ye, milord?"

"Sorry, Thomas; our job is to survive, as long as we can, and go on fighting."

"Where will't end? Stap me, 'tis as strange a maze as ever mortal man did tread!"

"I don't know; but as long as we're alive—and free—there's still a chance."

"The rogues o'ernumber us a thousand to our one; we'll but drown in a sea of 'em."

"Hold hard, there, mates," a Yankee seaman cut in. "Time to wear ship again, 'pears to me! Here comes Ben splittin' his skys'ls!"

I felt the vibration transmitted through the rock by hammering treads as the returning scout descended from the heights. He careened into view in the narrow way, braked to a halt in a shower of rock-chips.

"It's like you thought, Cap'n: we're flanked left and right—surrounded again," the Confederate cavalryman reported. "The other boys ain't much better off. Doubtsby's in a running fight to the southwest of us; he's lost fourteen men, and they're pushin' him hard. He's managed to pick up six recruits, but got no time to brief 'em. Joel's holed up in a small crater twenty mile north o' here; only twenty of his party got through, but he's picked up a bunch of new men, and he's freein' 'em as fast as he can. Bermuez is in trouble; he's surrounded, and takin' a poundin'; dunno how many he's lost."

"What are our chances of picking off some new men from here?"

"Too fur, Cap'n. I tried from the highest spot I could get to, and couldn't poke through the noise. The enemy's clamped down some kind o' rule agin' talkin', too; I think they're catchin' on that we been hearin' everthin' they say."

"What's the country like to the west of here, Ben?"

"Flat, mostly; a few bad draws. But they's heavy enemy concentration thataway."

My shrunken force of thirty units listened silently to the scout's report.

"We're losin'," someone said.

"The dropsy drown the hagseed," Thomas growled. "The devil take 'em by inchmeal."

I called for their attention. "So far we've had the

advantage of surprise," I said. "We've hit and run, done the unexpected; they've milled around us like a herd of buffalo. We've managed to slice through them, pick off a few isolated units, capture a few more. But the honeymoon is about over. They're standing off out of take-over range, and they've imposed communications silence, so we don't know what they're planning. They've caught onto the idea of flexible retreat before an inferior force, and they've contained two of our four detachments; three, if you count us. And it looks as though Doubtsby's not much better off."

"Like I said: we're losin'."

"Will we huddle here to be burned in our hall like Eric's men?" Aethelbert boomed. "Is this the tenth deed I'll relate to Thor in his mead-hall in Asgard?"

"We got to bust out of here," a Sixth Armored man said. "And fast, what I mean."

"We can keep hitting and running—and lose a few men each time," I went on. "In the end we'll be wiped out."

"In the name of the One God, let us carry the fight to the legions of Shaitan!"

"For the honor of the gods, I say attack!"

"We'll attack—but it will be a feint. Thomas, you'll take twenty-seven units, and move out to the south. Don't close; cruise their line at extreme range, as though you were looking for a weak spot. Put two of your best probemen on scan for recruits; you may be able to pick off a unit here and there. Keep up defensive fire only; if you draw out a pursuit column, fall back on this position, and try to capture them."

"Twenty-seven units say ye, sir? What of the others?"

"I'm taking two men. When you reach a point close to a two-seven-oh heading from here—turn and hit their line with everything you've got. That will be my signal to move out."

"Wi' two men only? By'r lakin, they'll trounce ye like a stockfish!"

"We'll come out with screens down, ports closed, and mingle with the enemy. In the confusion, I'm counting on their assuming we're loyal slaves. As soon as you see we're in their lines, turn and run for it. Keep them busy. With luck, we'll get through."

"And where would you be goin'?" an Irish voice demanded.

"Their headquarters is about twelve miles west of here. I'm going to try to reach it."

"And what will you do when you get there? I see no—"

"Avaunt, ye pied ninny! Would ye doubt our captain's wit?"

"Not I! But—"

"Then let be! Aye, Captain! We'll bear up and board 'em. We'll do our appointed office for stale, and putter out at three for one ye'll treble us o'er."

"To which of us falls the honor of your escort?" someone called.

A vast machine rumbled forward. "Who would take Aethelbert's place will fight for it!"

"Ye wouldn't think of tryin' it without me, Cap'n?" the scout Ben called.

"Ben and Aethelbert it is," I said. "Thomas, are you ready?"

"We'll go upright wi' our carriage, fear not, Cap'n! Now we'll avoid i' the instant."

"All right," I said. "Good luck to all of us; we'll need it."

With my two companions beside me, I waited at the south end of the ravine, watching the distant dust cloud that was Thomas' force as it raced across the starlit desert, the flickering of enemy guns lighting the scene with a winking radiance of blue and red and white.

"He'll be turning to hit them any minute," I said. "Remember the drill: communications silence, screens down, ports closed. If we're fired on, take evasive action, but don't return it."

"Hard will it be, and never gleeman's joywood will sing the deed," Aethelbert muttered. "By Odin's tree, the way of the hero is no easy one."

"Oh-oh," Ben said. "There they go!"

I saw the dust trail turn, drive for the massed loyalist units; the glow of gunfire brightened, concentrating. There was a general movement along the alien line as the forward ranks thrust out in flanking arms to enclose the attackers.

"Let's go!" I said. We moved out, raced toward the distant horizon behind which lay the Place That Must Be Defended. All around us, the high, grim shapes of enemy battle units loomed from the enveloping dust cloud, their guns ready, the baroque shapes of strange brigade markings gleaming on their sides. We rumbled steadily on, ignored in the churning confusion, altering course little by little to angle closer to our objective.

A unit with the garish markings of a Centurion turned across our path; its guns swung to track us. We trundled steadily on, steered past it. It moved off, and disappeared in the dust.

The number of loyalist units around us was lessening now; I increased speed, probing the opacity ahead with a focused radar beam. Moments later, the dust thinned. Abruptly we were in the open. I slammed full power to my drive mechanism, surged forward at a speed that made the landscape flash past in a blur of gray. The tall peak loomed, a mile or two ahead, and I saw now that the pass lay to the left of it. I flicked on a detector screen, fanned it out to scan the ground behind me. I saw a heavy machine roar out of the curtain of dust, its disrupter grid glowing a baleful red.

"They've spotted us!" I called. "Open fire—only a mile to go now!"

I heard Aethelbert and Ben's curt acknowledgments, felt the tremors in the rock that meant their heavy guns were firing. Another alien unit hurtled into view and opened fire.

On my left, Ben whooped suddenly, "I slipped home to him, Cap'n. Old Aethelbert was keepin' him busy, and I took him low. Watch!"

I saw the leading pursuer veer to the right, bound up a low slope, and smash headlong into a towering rock slab. There was a shock that lifted me clear of the ground, slammed me ahead; a fountain of molten chromalloy and rock leaped up, fell all around; then dust closed over the scene.

The pass was ahead now; I swung to enter it, gunned up the long slope. Ben followed, trailing by a quarter-mile. Far back, Aethelbert was coming up fast, the fire of the remaining alien unit lighting his defensive screens.

I reached the crest of the pass, came to a halt looking down on a vast complex of works—tunnel heads, squat sheds, low circular structures of unknown function—gray, rough-textured, stark and ugly against the bleakness of the lunar landscape. And beyond the warren of buildings, a tower reached up into the glittering black of the night sky, a ragged shape like a lone spire remaining from a fallen ringwall: the Place That Must Be Defended.

I looked back down the trail. From my vantage point I could see the broad sweep of the plain: the distant jumble of rock where we had regrouped, the milling mass of the enemy, strung out in a long pincers that enveloped the tiny group of winking lights that was Thomas and his dwindling band; and nearer, the dust trail reaching almost to the foot of the pass, and the second trail, close behind.

From halfway down the sloping trail, Ben called, "Aethelbert's in trouble; he's taken a hit, I think—and that fellow's closing on him. I better give him a leg up."

"Aethelbert!" I called. "Are you all right?"

There was no answer. I saw him slow as he entered the pass, then turn sideways, blocking the entry, his guns pointed toward the enemy. The oncoming unit poured fire into the now stationary target; it rocked to hit after hit. Ben, coming up beside me, swung his guns, opened fire on the alien unit as it came within range.

"Aethelbert, we'll cover you!" I called. "Come on up into the pass; you'll have shelter there!"

"I'll tarry here, Jones," came a faint reply. "There'll be no lack of foes to tempt my thunder."

"Just a few yards farther!"

"Bare is the back without brother behind it," he sang out. "Now take the mead-hall of the goblins by storm, and may Odin guide your sword-arm!"

"I'm goin' back for him!" Ben yelled.

"As you were, Ben! The target's ahead! Let's go and get it!" I launched myself down the slope without waiting to see him comply. A moment later, he passed me, racing to run interference.

"Head for the tower," I called. The first buildings were close now—unlovely constructions of featureless stone, puny in scale. I saw a tiny dark shape appear in a tunnel mouth, saw it bound toward a cluster of huts—and recognized it as one of the dog-things, looking no larger to me than a leaping rat, its head grotesquely muffled in a breathing mask—apparently its only protection from the lunar vacuum. I veered, bore down on it, saw its skull-face twist toward me as my treads caught it, pulped it in an instant, flung the bristled rag that was its corpse far behind.

Ben braked to a halt before a wide gate, swung his forward battery on it, blasted it to rubble, then roared ahead through the gap, with me close behind—

A shock wave struck me like a solid wall of steel. I felt myself go up, leap back, crash to the rocky ground, slide to rest in a shower of debris. Half dazed, I stared through the settling dust, saw the blackened hulk that had been my Confederate scout, smoke boiling from every aperture, his treads gone, gun barrels melted. I shouted his name, caught a faint reply:

"Cap'n ... don't move ... trap ... all automatic stuff. I saw 'em ... too late. Hellbores ... set in the walls. You'll trigger 'em ... when you move ... don't ... stir...." I felt his mind-field fade, wink out.

I scanned the interior of the compound, saw the black mouths of the mighty guns, aimed full on me—waiting. I reached out, felt for the dim glow of cybernetic controls, but found nothing. They were mechanically operated, set to blast anything that moved in the target area. The detonation that had halted me in my tracks had saved my life.

Ben was dead. Behind me, Aethelbert held the pass alone, and on the plain, my comrades fought on, in ever-dwindling numbers, covering my desperate bid for victory.

And I was here, caught like a fly in a web—helpless, fifty yards from my objective.

Chapter Sixteen

The explosion had blackened the pavement of the court, gouged a crater a yard deep, charred the blank invulnerable walls that ringed it. My hull, too, must be blackened and pitted. I could see fragments of my blasted comrade scattered all across the yard; splashes of molten metal were bright against the drab masonry.

There were openings in the walls, I noted as the last of the dust fell back, and the final shreds of black smoke dissipated in the near-vacuum. They seemed no bigger than ratholes, but I realized they were actually about a yard wide and half again as high.

As I watched, a pale snout poked from one; then the lean withers and flanks of a demon appeared, its size diminished by contrast with my immense body. The thing wore a respirator helmet like the one I had seen earlier; straps crisscrossed its back. It bounded lightly to the burned-out hulk of Ben's body. It circled, stepping daintily around chunks that still glowed red. It came across to me, then disappeared as it passed under the range of my visual sensors.

I held myself motionless, carefully withdrew vitality from my external circuitry, closed myself behind an inner shield of no-thought. Alone in the absolute darkness of sensory deprivation, I waited for what might happen next.

Faintly, I felt a probing touch—ghostly fingers of alien thought that groped along my dark circuits, seeking indications of activity. There was an abortive shudder as an impulse was directed at my drive controls. Then the probe withdrew.

Cautiously, I extended sensitivity to my visual complex, saw the creature as it trotted back to its hole. Again the compound was silent and empty, except for the corpse of the great machine that had been my friend.

Quickly, I ran an inspection, and discovered the worst: my drive mechanism was fused at vital points in the front suspension, and my forward batteries were inoperative—warped by the terrific heat of the blast from the hellbores that had smashed Ben. I was trapped inside ten thousand terrestrial tons of inert, dead metal.

More demons emerged from the building, trotting from the same arched doorway. Other creatures followed—squat, many-armed things like land-walking octopi. They went to Ben, swarmed over the hot metal. Perched high on the blackened carapace, they set to work. Below on the dusty ground, the demons paced, or stood in pairs, silently watching.

I considered reaching out to touch a demon mind, and rejected the idea. I was not skilled enough to be sure of not alerting it, warning it that something still lived inside my scorched and battered hull.

Instead, I selected a small horror squatting on

the fused mass that had been Ben's forward turret; I reached out, found the awareness-center . . .

Grays and blacks and whites, dimly seen, but with distorted pseudoscent images sharp-etched; furtive thoughts of food and warmth and rest; a wanderlust, and a burning drive for a formless concept that was a female . . .

It was the brain of a cat, installed in the maintenance machine, its natural drives perverted to the uses of the aliens. I explored the tiny brain, and saw the wonderful complexity of even this simple mechanism—vastly more sophisticated than even the most complex of cybernetic circuits.

With an effort, I extended the scope of my contact, saw mistily what the cat-machine saw: the pitted surface of metal on which it squatted, the tiny cutting tools with which it was drilling deep into the burned chromalloy of the ruined hull. I sensed the heat of the metal, the curve of it under me, the monomaniacal drive to do thus—and thus—boring the holes, setting the charge, moving on to the next. . . .

I pulled back, momentarily confused by the immediacy of the experience. The small machines, under the direction of the demons, were preparing to blast open the fused access hatch.

Abruptly, I became aware of a sensation in my outer hull, checked the appropriate sensors, felt the pressure of small bodies, the hot probe of needle-tipped drills . . .

In my preoccupation, I had failed to notice that a crew was at work on me, too. In minutes, or at most in an hour or two, a shock would drive through me, as my upper access hatch was blasted away, exposing my living brain to the vacuum and the cold metal probes of the machines.

I reached out to the maintenance unit again. I insinuated myself into its cramped ego center, absorbed its self-identity concept, felt for and made

contact with its limited senses, its multiple limbs—
analogous, I discovered, to fingers and toes.

Now I seemed to squat high on the ruined machine, looking across with dim sight at the towering fire-scarred hulk that was myself. My entire
forward surface was a fused mass, deeply indented
by the force of the explosion. One tread was stripped
away, and the proud barrels of my infinite re-
peater battery were charred stumps, protruding
from the collapsed shape of their turret. Busy workers were dark shapes like fat spiders on the towering hulk of my body.

Delicately, I directed movement to the cat's limbs.
They moved smoothly in response, walked me
across the twisted metal. I turned the sensory cluster to stare across at the openings in the wall,
gaping now like great arched entries. Half a dozen
now-huge demons paced or stood between me and
the doors. None seemed to have noticed that I was
no longer at work. I moved on down the side of the
wrecked machine, sprang to the dust-drifted ground.
A demon turned empty red eyes on me, looked
past me, turned aside. I moved toward the nearest
archway, scuttling along at a speed that I hoped
was appropriate to a maintenance unit returning
to its storage bay for repairs or supplies.

Another demon swung its head to watch, followed me with its eyes as I crossed the open
ground. I reached the doorway, hopped up the low
step, slipped into the darkness of the high-arched
passage.

Here I turned, looked back, and caught a last
glimpse of the mighty machine that had been my
body. Inside it, in a trance-like state, my brain still
lay—helpless now, vulnerable to any attack, mental or physical, that might be directed against it.
The least probe from a curious demon, a command
from a Centurion, and I would fall once again
under the spell that had held me before—but this

time, there would be no reserve personality fraction to preserve me.

And the fragment of the living force that was a mind-field, detached and localized in the intricacy of the brain of a cat—the intangible that was the essential 'I'—was helpless too, defenseless without the power of the native brain to draw on.

But somewhere in the ominous tower before me—the Place That Must Be Defended—lay the secret of the power of the demons. I started into the dark maze.

The passage was featureless, unadorned, running straight to a heavy lock that opened at the pulse my well-drilled cat-brain emitted. I scuttled forward into a tiny chamber, waited while the inner seal slid aside. A wider corridor lay before me, brightly illuminated in the infra-red range, and crowded with hurrying demons, looking as immense as gaunt and bristled horses.

I moved ahead, ignored by the busy inmates of the building. I found a rising ramp, hurried up its wide curve, and emerged on another level. It was like the first, except that there were other creatures here—tall, mechanical-looking things that ambled on iridescent chitinous limbs. I saw one or two demons of another species, characterized by flatter faces, enormous protruding teeth, and pale, tawny hides. They wore more elaborate harness than the worker-class things I had met in the past, and there was a glint of jeweled decoration on their brightwork fittings—the first signs of vanity I had seen among the aliens.

I saw two of the humanoid aliens of the General Julius type. Both wore familiar earthly costumes—one a pink business suit and the other a stained military uniform; I judged they were agents reporting on their operations among the natives. None of these varied life-forms paid the slightest attention to me, but I couldn't help feeling as vulnerable as a newborn mouse in a rattler's cage.

Moving past a congregation of the insect-things before a wide, square-cut door, I spied a narrow stair leading up from a short passage to the right. I turned it, went along to it, looked up its dark well. What I was looking for, I didn't know—but instinct seemed to urge me upward. I hopped up with my ten legs and began the climb.

I was in a wide chamber with a high ceiling supported by columns, among which massive apparatus was ranked in endless rows. Great red-eyed demons prowled the aisles beside stilt-legged insect-things—whether as guards or servants, I couldn't tell. A cacophony of humming, buzzing, raucous squealing, deep-toned roaring, filled the thin air, as the batteries of giant machines churned out their unimaginable products. I scurried along, darting around the careless footfalls of the giant creatures. I made for a door across the room, on either side of which two immense demons squatted on their haunches like vast watchdogs. I thought of the soldier in the fairy-tale, who had stolen the treasure guarded by a dog with eyes as big as saucers. These eyes were smaller, and of a baleful red, but they were as watchful as lookouts for a burglar gang. They were guarding something; that was reason enough for me to want to pass the door.

I scurried past them, saw other small machines like myself hurrying about their tasks, numbly skipping aside when threatened by heavy feet. I had chosen my disguise well: the tiny cat-brained devices appeared to have free run of the tower.

There was a quiet corner where a cross-aisle dead-ended. I settled myself in it, blanked off sensory input. I reached out to the most superficial level of mental activity, and sensed the darting action-reaction impulses of the other cat-brains all around me. I selected one dim center, felt gingerly through its simple drives. I selected one, stimulated it, planted a concept. Quickly I jumped to a second brain, keyed its elemental impulses, then went on to a fourth, and a fifth . . .

I withdrew, focused my sensors. Across the floor, I saw a small machine darting erratically about, attracting cold stares from the busy creatures around it. A second machine scuttled into view from between giant mechanisms, paused a moment, jittering on thin legs, then darted to the first, leaped at it. With a metallic clatter, the two rolled across the floor, struck the lean shank of a demon that bounded aside, whirled, struck out.

A third cat-brained machine dashed to join the fray; two more appeared at the same moment, saw each other, came together with a crash—five enraged toms, each sure he was attacking a rival for the imagined female the image of whose presence I had evoked—a dirty trick but effective.

The two guardian demons bounded from their posts, sprang at the combatants, cuffed them apart—but only for an instant. Nimbly, the fighting cats danced aside from the rush of the dog-things, darted back to re-engage.

I moved from my corner, scurried along the baseboard to the guarded door, fired a triggering pulse at its mechanism. It stood firm. I extended a sensing probe. I perceived the required form for the unlocking signal, transmitted it. The moronic apparatus responded, withdrew the magnetic locking field. I nudged the door, felt it swing open. I slipped past it, and pushed it shut behind me.

A narrow stairwell led up toward light. I started up, feeling my thin limbs tiring now. My power-pack needed recharging; I felt a powerful reflexive urge to descend to a dimly-conceived place where a niche waited, where I could snuggle against com-

forting contacts and receive a pleasure-flow of renewed vitality . . .

I overrode the conditioned urge, clambered up
the high-looming steps. They were scaled to the
long legs of the demons, almost too high for my
limited agility. There was no alarm from below;
the demon-guardians had failed to notice the pen-
etration of their sanctum.

I reached a landing, started up a second flight.
The top of the tower had to be close now, judging
from the distance I had come. The light ahead
beckoned . . . only a little farther . . .

I dragged myself up over the last step. I was
looking into a round room, walled with nacreous
material like mother-of-pearl, with glazed openings beyond which the black lunar sky pressed
close. At the center of the chamber, a shallow bowl
rested on a short column, like a truncated bird-
bath of polished metal.

After a moment's rest, I moved into the room. I
was aware of a curious humming, a sense of vast
power idling at the edge of perceptibility. The floor
was smooth under me, extending to a curving join
with the walls, which rose, darkening, to form a
shadowed dome many yards overhead. The light
was diffuse and soft. I circled the gleaming pedestal, searching for some indication of the meaning
or utility of this strange place, so unlike the functional ugliness of the levels below. There was
nothing—no indication of life, no sign of controls
or instrumentation. Perhaps, after all, the Place
That Must Be Defended was no more than a tem-
ple dedicated to whatever strange deities might
command the devotion of the monsters that prowled
the levels below. . . .

There was a sound—a dry clicking, like a dead
twig tapping a window. I crouched near the pedestal, stared around me. I saw nothing. The walls of
the empty room gleamed softly.

The sound came again—then a dry squeaking, as of leather sliding against bare metal. A diffuse shadow, faint, formless, glided down the walls. I turned my sensors upward—and saw it.

It hung in the gloom of the dome, a bulging, grayish body in a cluster of tentacular members like giant angleworms, clinging to a bright filament depending from the peak of the onion-shaped dome. As I watched, it dropped down another foot, its glistening reticulated arms moving with a hideous, fluid grace. A cluster of stemmed sense organs poked from the upper side of the body—crab-eyes on a torso like a bag of oil. I recognized the shape of the creature; it was the one on which my borrowed mechanical form was modeled.

The thing saw me then—I was sure of it. It paused in its descent, tilted its eyes toward me. I didn't move. Then the worm-arms twitched, flowed; it dropped lower, unreeling the cable as it came. It was five yards above the parabolic bowl, then four, then three. There was a feeling of haste in its movements now, something frantic in its scrambling descent. Whatever the thing was, its objective was clear: to reach the polished bowl before I did.

I sprang to the pedestal and reared up, my forelimbs catching at the edge of the bowl. I scrabbled with other legs at the smooth base, found purchase for another pair of limbs; I was clear of the floor now, rising to the edge—

The thing above me emitted a mewing cry, dropped abruptly another yard, then released its support and launched itself at me; the flailing tentacles wrapped me in an embrace like a nest of constrictors. I lost my hold, fell back with a stunning crash. The alien thing broke away, reached for the bowl, and swung itself up. I sprang after it, seized a trailing limb with three of mine and hauled back. It turned like a striking snake, struck out at

me—blows that sent me over on my back, skidding away, until I was brought up short by the
grip I had retained on one outflung member. I
righted myself with a bound, crouched under a
new rain of blows. I lashed out in return, saw
thick mustard-colored fluid ooze from a wound on
the heavy body.

The thing went mad; it lashed its many legs in
wild, unaimed blows, leaping against the restraint
of my grip. I caught another flailing arm, the cruel
metal of my pincers biting into muscle. Abruptly
it changed its tactics: its multiple arms reached
out to me, seized me, hauled me close; then, with
a surge, it raised me and dashed me down against
the rock-hard floor.

Dazed, I felt my grip go slack. The sinuous members of the alien withdrew. I reached after it, felt a
last member slither from my weakened grasp.

I could see again. The thing was at the pedestal,
swarming up, teetering on the edge of the bowl. I
gathered my strength and lunged after it—drove
my outstretched arm up at the unprotected under-
body, felt it strike, pierce deep . . .

The thing wailed, a horrifying cry; for a moment, it wrapped its futile arms around my stabbing metal one; then it went limp, fell back, struck
and lay, a slack heap of flabby, colorless flesh, in a
spatter of viscous ochre.

I rested for a moment, feeling the on-off-on flashes
of failing senses. I had spent the last of my waning
energy in the battle with the deciped. It was hard
to hold my grip on the fading consciousness of the
cat-brain; almost, I could feel my awareness slipping away, back to the doomed hulk in the court-
yard below. I wondered how close the drillers were
now to the vulnerable brain—and how Aethelbert
fared at the pass, how many of my comrades still
lived on the battlefield beyond.

There was one more thing required of me before I fell back into the darkness. I dragged myself to the base of the pedestal, rose up, tottering, groped for the edge. It was too far. I sank back quivering, black lights dancing in my dimming sensory field. Beside me lay the dead alien. I groped to it, crawled up on the slumped curve of its body, tried again. Now my forelimbs reached the edge of the bowl, gripped; I pushed myself up, brought other limbs into play. Now I swung, suspended; with a final effort, I hauled myself up, groped, found a hold across the bowl—and tipped myself into the polished hollow.

From a source as bottomless as space itself, power flowed, sweeping through me with an ecstasy that transcended pleasure, burning away the dead husks of fatigue, hopelessness, pain. I felt my mind come alive, as a thousand new senses illuminated the plane of spacetime in which I hung; I sensed the subtle organizational patterns of the molecular aggregations that swirled over me, the play of oscillations all across the spectrum of electromagnetic radiation, the infinity of intermeshing pressures, flows, transitions that were reality.

The scope of my awareness spread out to sense the structured honeycomb of the tower walls, the scurrying centers of energy that were living minds nested in flesh and metal; it drove outward to embrace the surrounding court, noting the bulk of cold metal in which my unconscious brain lay buried—and outward still, sweeping across the curve of the world, detecting the patterned network of glowing points scattered across the waste of lifelessness.

Now each dim radiance took on form and dimension, swelling until its inner structures lay exposed. I saw the familiar forms of human minds, each locked in a colorless prison of paralysis—and the alien shapes of demon-minds, webs of weird thought-forms born of an unknowable conception of reality. And here and there, in clusters, were other minds, beacons of flashing vitality—the remnants of my fighting Brigades. I singled out one, called to it:

"JOEL! HOW DOES THE FIGHT GO?"

His answer was a flare of confusion, question; then:

"They're poundin' us, Jones. Where are you? Can you send us any help?"

"HOLD ON, JOEL! I'M IN THEIR HEADQUARTERS. I'LL DO WHAT I CAN!"

"You gave me a turn, Jones. For a minute I thought you was the Over-mind, you came through so strong." His voice was fading. *"I guess it'll all be over pretty soon, Jones. I'm glad we tried, though. Sorry it turned out like this . . ."*

"DON'T GIVE UP—NOT YET!" I broke off, scanned again the array of enslaved human minds. I thought back to the frantic hour I had spent when Joel and I had freed the trapped minds of Aethelbert and Doubtsby and Bermuez ... If I could reach them all now, in one great sweep—

I brought the multitude of dully glowing centers into sharp focus, fixed in my mind the pattern of their natural resonance—and sent out a pulse.

All across the dark face of the dead world, faint points of illumination quickened, flared up, blazed bright. At once, I fired an orientation-concept—a single complex symbol that placed in each dazed and newly-emancipated brain the awareness of the status quo, the need for instant attack on demon-brained enemies.

I switched my plane of reference back to Joel.

"HOLD YOUR FIRE!" I called. "BE ON THE ALERT FOR NEW RECRUITS COMING OVER, BY THE FULL BRIGADE!"

I caught Joel's excited answer, then switched to

Doubtsby, told him what had happened, went on to alert the others.

The pattern of the great battle changed. Now isolated demon-brained machines fought furiously against overwhelming odds, winked out one by one. Far away, in distant depots, on planet-lit deserts a thousand miles from the tower of the Overmind, awakened slave Brigades blasted astonished Centurions, sallied forth to seek out and destroy the hated former masters.

From a dozen hidden fortresses, beleaguered demons fitted out vast siege units, sent them forth to mow broad swathes through the attacking battle units before they fell to massive bombardments. In a lull, I searched through the building below me, found and pinched out the frantic demons hiding there. Their numbers dwindled, shrank from thousands to a dozen, six, two, a single survivor—then none.

The moon was ours.

Chapter Seventeen

Joel's great bulk, pitted with new scars bright against the old, loomed up beside me in the compound.

"All the fellows are here now, Jones—we lost seventy-one, the Major says. A couple dozen more are disabled, like you and Aethelbert, but still alive. The maintenance machines have gone to work on 'em. We got plenty of spares, anyway. We'll have you rolling again in no time."

"Good work, Joel." I widened my contact to take in all of the hundred and eight intact survivors of the original group of freed slaves.

"Every one of you will have his hands full, rounding up the new men and organizing them. We have no way of knowing how soon our late enemies' home base will start inquiring after them—and when they do, we want to be ready."

"What about going home, chief?" called a man who had taken a bullet in the knee at the Hurtgen Forest. "How we going to get back?"

"You off your onion, mate?" a one-time British sailor growled. "What kind o' show you think we'd make waltzing into Piccadilly in these get-ups?"

"We got to go back, to kill off the rest of these devils, haven't we?"

"Mum, my masters," Thomas interrupted. "Hear out our captain."

"Two days ago I used the aliens' equipment to call Earth," I told them. "I managed a link-up to the public visiscreen system, and got through to the Central Coordinating Monitor of an organization called the Ultimax Group. I gave them the full picture; they knew what to do. The aliens are outnumbered a million to one down there; a few thousand troops wearing special protective helmets and armed with recoil-less rifles can handle them."

"Yeah, but what about us?" the soldier burst out. "What are we going to do—stay on this godforsaken place forever? Hell, there's transports at the depots; let's use 'em! I got a wife and kids back there!"

"Art daft, fellow?" a dragoon of Charles the Second inquired. "Your chicks are long since dust, and their dam with them—as are mine, God pity 'em."

"My old woman's alive and cursing yet, no doubt," said a Dutch UN platoon leader. "But she wouldn't know me now—and keeping me in reaction mass'd play hell with her household budget. No, I can't see going back."

"Maybe—they could get us human bodies again, some way . . ."

"Human body, indeed!" the dragoon cut him off. "Could a fighting man hope for a better corpse than this, that knows naught of toothache, the ague nor the French disease?"

Another voice cut into the talk—the voice of Ramon Descortes of the Ultimax Group, listening in from Earth on the circuit I held open.

"General Bravais," he said excitedly—and I channeled his transmission through my circuitry, broadcasting it to every man within range—"I've been following your talk, and although I find it unbelievable, I'm faced with the incontrovertible evidence. Our instruments indicate that your transmissions are undoubtedly coming from outside the Solar System—how and why you will explain in due course, I hope. You've told me that you and the others have been surgically transplanted into robot bodies. Now you wish to be restored, naturally. Let me urge you to return—and we will have for each of you a new body of superb design—not strictly human, admittedly—but serviceable, to say the least!"

I had to call for order to quell the uproar.

"Some kind of android?" I asked.

"We have on hand a captive—an alien operative of the humanoid type. We will capture more—alive. They will be anesthetized and placed in deep freeze, awaiting your return. According to the present estimate, there are some ten thousand of them working here on Earth—sufficient for your needs, I believe."

"Say, how's the fight going there?" someone called.

"Well. The first Special Units have gone into action at Chicago, Paris, and Tamboula, with complete success. Governments are falling like autumn leaves, well-known figures are suiciding in droves, and mad dogs are reported everywhere. It is only a matter of hours now."

"Then—there's nothing to stand in the way—"

"Broadway, here I come—"

"Paris—without a king? Why—"

"An end to war? As well an end to living—"

"What about you, General?" someone called, and others joined in.

"I'll order the transports made ready immediately," I said. "Every man that wants to go back can leave in a matter of hours."

"Jones—I mean, General—" Joel started.

"Jones will do; I won't need the old name any more."

"You're not going back?"

"We fought a battle here," I said. "And we won. But the war goes on—on a hundred worlds; a thousand—we don't know how many. The demons rule space—but Man is on his way now. He'll be jumping off Earth, reaching out to those worlds. And when he reaches them—he'll find the armored brigades of the aliens waiting for him. Nothing can stand against them—except us. We've proved that we can outfight twice our number in slave machines—and we can free the minds that control those machines, turn them against the aliens. The farther we go, the bigger our force will be. Some day, in the far future, we'll push them off the edge of the galaxy. Until then, the war goes on. I can't go home again—but I *can* fight for home, wherever I find the enemy."

"General Bravais," a new voice cut in. "Surely you can't mean that? Why, your name will be on every tongue on Earth! You're the hero of the century—of any century! You'll be awarded every decoration—"

"A battle-scarred five-thousand-ton battle unit would be ill at ease in a procession down Pennsylvania Avenue," I said. "For better or worse, my chromalloy body and I are joined. Even if I had a human body again, I couldn't sit on a veranda and sip a whisky sour, knowing what was waiting—out there. So I'm going to meet it, instead. How many are going with me?"

And the answer was a mighty roar in many tongues, from many ages—the voice of Man, that would soon be heard among the stars.

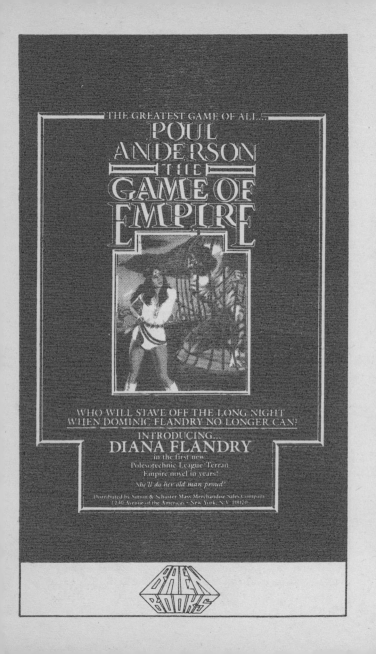

HAVE YOU FOUND YOURSELF ENJOYING A LOT OF BAEN BOOKS LATELY?

We at Baen Books like science fiction with real science in it and fantasy that reaches to the heart of the human soul—and we think a lot of you do, too. Why not let us know? We'll award $25 and a dozen Baen paperbacks of your choice to the reader who best tells us what he or she likes about Baen Books. We reserve the right to quote any or all of you...and we'll feature the best quote in an advertisement in <u>American Bookseller</u> and other magazines! Contest closes March 15, 1986. All letters should be addressed to Baen Books, 8 W. 36th St., New York, N.Y. 10018.

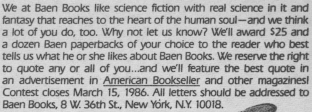

PATRICK TILLEY
CLOUD WARRIOR

"Reminiscent of Stephen King's *The Stand*." — *Fantasy Review*

"Technology, magic, sex and excitement. . .when the annual rite of selection for the Hugos and Nebulas comes around, CLOUD WARRIOR is a good bet to be among the top choices." — *San Diego Union*

"A real page-turner!" — *Publishers Weekly*

Two centuries after the holocaust, the survivors are ready to leave their underground fortress and repossess the Blue Sky World. Its inhabitants have other ideas....

352 pp. • $3.50